WORLD

CHANGINGUNIVERSE

WORLD

Terrance Dicks

Piccadilly Press • London

CHANGINGUNIVERSE

Printed and bound by WBC, Bridgend,
for the publishers Piccadilly Press Ltd,
5 Castle Road, London NW1 8PR

A catalogue record for this book is available from
the British Library

ISBNs: 1 85340 536 1 (trade paperback)
1 85340 531 0 (hardback)

Terrance Dicks lives in North London.
He has written many books for Piccadilly Press including
THE UNEXPLAINED series,
the CHRONICLES OF A COMPUTER GAME ADDICT series,
the HARVEY series
and THE GOOD, THE BAD AND THE GHASTLY series.

Cover photographs © Superstock, 1998
Design by Judith Robertson
Cover design by Mandy Sherliker

TRANSMAT

IT BEGAN as a routine journey for Tom and Sarah.

It ended as a nightmare.

They'd been for a weekend's sightseeing in New York and now they were on their way home to London.

'Looks like a good day to go home,' yelled Tom, as they dashed along the rain-lashed streets between their hotel and the transmat depot.

New York had been hit by a sudden freak thunderstorm. Lightning flashed across the dark skies between the skyscrapers, thunder rolled and rain poured down in the narrow valleys between the tall buildings.

Tom and Sarah ducked into the big Central Transmat Depot – it had once been Grand Central Station – relieved to be out of the downpour.

The queues for the hundreds of transmat booths surrounding the huge concourse weren't too long at this time of day. In a matter of minutes they'd be back home in London.

Tom, as usual, found something to grumble about.

'Everything's too instant these days,' he muttered as they waited in front of one of the booths.

Sarah gave him a quizzical look. 'Now what?'

'Not so long ago we'd have had a relaxing six or seven hours in a plane before we got home.'

Sarah yawned. 'What a ghastly thought!'

'Before that we'd have had a nice sea cruise to look forward to,' said Tom. 'Five days on an ocean liner.'

'Five days of storms and seasickness!' said Sarah scornfully.

'It's all too easy these days,' grumbled Tom. 'We step into a transmat booth, shove a credit card in a slot, dial a few coordinates and bingo, we're back home!'

Sarah shook her head. 'I don't know, Tom. You and your history. Only you could be nostalgic for all the problems of the past!'

All the same, she thought, it was pretty amazing how quickly the matter transporter – the transmat as it was called – had changed the world.

It had been demonstrated first in the year 2008, an exciting new exhibit in the Millennium Science Pavilion.

Sarah's father had visited it as a young man, and seen one of the first demonstrations. The astonished audience had watched as a variety of objects – a silver cup, a coffee pot, a paper-wrapped parcel of books – faded away from beneath one glass dome to reappear in another, some twenty metres away.

The grand finale had been the transference of a placid white rabbit and a squawking duck in exactly the same way.

At first people assumed it was some kind of conjuring trick, an optical illusion. But the scientists running the demonstration showed conclusively that everything was exactly as it seemed.

Matter transmission, so long confined to science fiction shows – 'Beam me up, Scotty!' – had become science fact. The molecules composing a solid object, even those of a living being, could be broken down, transmitted through space – or through some mysterious other dimension – and reassembled somewhere else.

Nobody seemed quite sure exactly how the transmat worked. Even the scientists who'd invented it argued amongst themselves. But the fact remained that it did work – and it had changed the world.

Once the principle was established, its practical development was only a matter of time. A year later the process was working efficiently over virtually any distance. Goods could be transmitted instantly, anywhere in the world.

The next stage was the transmission of human beings. This seemed to be a lot trickier at first and there were strange tales of mysterious disappearances.

By now the big corporations were pouring millions into transmat research and the problems were very soon ironed out. Before long the transmission of humans became possible. In time, it became routine. The changes to society were immense.

Now that both goods and people could be moved reliably and inexpensively by transmat, road, rail and air travel became a thing of the past. These days, seven short years after transmat's first appearance, you went to a transmat station and despatched yourself to the terminal nearest your destination.

Once there, seconds later, you took an electric tram or an electric runabout for the last stages of your journey.

Much of the world's pollution problems simply disappeared, and the scientists said that even global warming was slowing down.

The car didn't disappear completely, of course. Like the steam train of the previous century it was preserved by a few die-hard enthusiasts. But in the year 2015 driving a car was like riding a horse – something you did purely for the fun of it.

Tom, who was interested in all aspects of the past, was a keen internal combustion fan. He attended rallies where you could drive old automobiles on private roads or abandoned airfields, and soon became an expert driver.

Sarah had grown up with the transmat. Now, in 2015, she took it completely for granted, just like everyone else.

Sarah and Tom were first cousins – their fathers were brothers and their mothers were sisters.

When Sarah's parents died in one of the last plane crashes Tom's family had taken her in, and they had been brought up like brother and sister.

Despite her family tragedy, Sarah grew up lively, cheerful and outgoing, the sort of girl who made friends easily.

Tom, however, was occasionally moody and often reserved. He had a sharp tongue and an ironic sense of humour.

Despite their differences, Tom and Sarah preferred spending time with each other than with anyone else. They didn't have to bother making a good impression, or worry about hurting each other's feelings. They often seemed to know what the other was thinking.

The traveller before them in the queue was an impressive-looking Indian businessman in a dark suit. He carried an expensive briefcase and wore an immaculate white turban. He stepped into the transmat booth, inserted his card and entered some coordinates.

The glass-walled booth lit up and the Indian gentleman faded away, to reappear, presumably, in Karachi or Bombay. No doubt he'd just popped over for a quick conference.

The booth darkened again and Sarah stepped forward.

Tom touched her arm. 'Hang on a second.'

'Why? The booth's free.'

'I always like to leave a little gap between transmat journeys.'

'Whatever for?'

'Something might go wrong. I don't want my molecules mixed up with someone else's.'

'Idiot!' Sarah opened the booth door and stepped inside, pulling Tom after her. 'Nothing can go wrong with transmat, everyone knows that!'

Sarah produced her Cred card and put it in the slot. When the machine whirred and clicked its approval she took out the card and dialled a complicated set of coordinates on the big keyboard in front of her.

Tom always left this sort of thing to Sarah. As a history student he liked to pretend that modern technology baffled him. Sarah, who was more of a scientist, said he was just lazy.

'Hope you got those right,' grumbled Tom. 'When you rattle the coordinates off from memory like that I'm always worried we're going to end up in Wogga Wogga or Timbuctoo.'

'We'll end up in the Trafalgar Square terminal, same as usual,' said Sarah confidently.

She was quite right – in a way.

A jagged streak of lightning flashed across the sky above Central Transmat Depot, followed by a thunderclap so loud that it shook the building.

In the huge circular control room beneath the building a nervous young transmat technician stared hard at his monitor screen. It was his first day on the job and he didn't want to make a fool of himself. All the same . . .

A supervisor appeared at his shoulder. 'Something wrong?'

'I thought I saw a blip in my section, sir. Booth 347.'

The supervisor studied the screen. 'I don't see anything.'

'Nor do I, sir, now. It seems to have corrected itself.'

'Is the booth operational?'

'Yes, sir. A double transmission to London, England is underway.'

'There you are, then.'

'Yes, sir, but . . .'

'But what?'

'Shouldn't I report it?'

'Report what?' said the supervisor blandly. 'Nothing happened, did it?'

'I suppose not, sir.'

'So – there's nothing to report.'

'No, sir.'

'Carry on.'

The supervisor nodded and strolled away. The boy would soon learn. Occasionally, very occasionally, some kind of blip did occur on the transmat system. With millions of travellers every day these things were inevitable.

But it didn't do to dwell on them. No need to alarm the paying public . . .

STRANGE ARRIVAL

DURING THE brief transmat transmission, Tom was still brooding on the monotony of modern life.

For example, all transmat journeys were exactly the same.

The booth lit up, and you closed your eyes . . .

A few seconds of disorientation, and you opened them again. You were still in a transmat booth.

Only this transmat booth could be in another city or another country. It could be on the other side of the world.

Even as he was thinking these thoughts Tom became aware that this particular transmat journey *was* different. It seemed to be going on longer and the feeling of disorientation was far stronger.

He felt Sarah grip his arm and heard her alarmed voice.

'Tom? Tom, what's happening?'

The glow faded and things seemed to return to normal.

'It's all right,' said Tom, a little unsteadily. 'We've arrived.'

They looked around, pleased to find themselves in the familiar surroundings of a transmat booth.

Only it wasn't quite the usual design of transmat booth.

It was larger and more luxurious and the console was decorated with a strange-looking crooked cross.

Sarah shook her head. 'That felt – weird.'

'Maybe the storm affected transmission,' said Tom. 'Anyway, we're here now.'

They stepped out of the booth.

Sarah looked around. 'We're here all right – but where?'

'We've come to the wrong place,' said Tom. 'I thought you said transmat never went wrong?'

They should have been in the familiar Trafalgar Square terminal, by the side of the old National Gallery.

But this terminal was different. It was smaller, with only a handful of transmat booths. It was luxurious too, with marble floors and walls. Strangest of all, it was empty.

'We seem to have arrived in some kind of VIP area,' said Sarah. 'We'd better clear out before we find ourselves in trouble.'

An arched doorway led out of the little terminal. They could see a short corridor beyond.

Suddenly a man in a black uniform appeared, hurrying

down the corridor towards them. He had heavy, brutal features and he had a holstered pistol at his belt.

He was a sinister, frightening figure and Sarah saw that Tom was staring at him in horrified disbelief.

'Oh no,' he whispered. 'It can't be . . .'

'Can't be what?'

'SS,' muttered Tom.

Sarah didn't know what he was talking about.

The man's manner, when he reached them, couldn't have been more respectful. He was positively grovelling.

'Your pardon, excellencies,' he said breathlessly. 'I was not told to expect any arrivals . . .'

He broke off, staring at them in amazement.

It was quite obvious that they were not what he was expecting to see. His respectful manner disappeared and his tone became harsh and suspicious.

'Who are you? What are you doing here?'

'We just – arrived,' said Sarah.

'This terminal is reserved for the exclusive use of Party officials.' The man's hand went to the revolver in his belt. 'Tell me quickly, who are you and how did you get in here? Answer, or you'll be sorry.'

To Sarah's amazement Tom snapped, 'I advise you to change your tone, or you'll be the one who's sorry.'

The man gaped at him.

'This terminal is reserved for high-ranking Party officials,' said Tom. 'And we've just arrived in it.'

'There is no proof that . . .'

Tom glared at the guard. 'So, what does that make us? It makes us Party officials doesn't it?'

'But, so young . . .'

'Don't be stupid, man. How else would we be here?'

Sarah didn't really know what was going on, but she decided to join in anyway. 'Appearance isn't everything. We may not be as young as we look.'

Before the man could answer, Tom snapped, 'We are here on urgent Party business. Urgent and secret. Show us to the nearest exit – quickly, now!'

The man led them down the corridor, unlocked a heavy door, stood aside and came to attention, raising his arm in salute.

'Now, remember,' said Tom sternly. 'Our business is secret. Say nothing to anyone.'

He waved Sarah through the door and then followed her. The door slammed behind them.

They found themselves on a broad pavement in the open air, in front of an official-looking building.

Sarah turned to Tom. 'What was all that about?'

Tom's face was grim. 'The man was a bully. One of the best ways to deal with bullies is to bully them!'

'Who did he think he was, talking to us like that?' said Sarah indignantly. 'And where are we anyway? We must have arrived at the wrong terminal. Tom?'

Tom didn't answer. He was looking around him.

Sarah looked too and gave a gasp of amazement, her questions forgotten.

They were standing in Trafalgar Square – but it was a very different square from the one they knew.

Some of the old familiar buildings were still there – the National Gallery, St Martin-in-the-Fields. Others, like the old South Africa House, had been replaced by new ones. New, but somehow not modern. These were huge civic buildings, all built in marble in the most magnificent style.

Tall pillars, towering columns, paved courtyards, fountains and colonnades . . .

Something large, noisy and smelly roared past and Sarah jumped back, choking on its fumes. 'What was that?'

'Traffic,' said Tom grimly. 'Wherever we are, they're still using motor cars.'

Other vehicles sped round the square, most of them long and black and shiny.

'Tom, look at the people,' whispered Sarah.

Lots of people were hurrying around the square, getting in and out of cars, entering and leaving the different buildings. Many of them were in uniform. Most of the uniforms were black, with a smattering of grey and brown.

Uniformed or not, everyone seemed to be marching about with an air of brisk efficiency.

No one was smiling.

'Where are we?' said Sarah. 'What's happened?'

'The transmat's malfunctioned,' said Tom. 'But what's going on . . . ?'

'There were a lot of weird theories in the early days,' said Sarah. 'Some people thought the transmat might send you to the future – or to the past. Maybe we're in the past. After all, if they're still using the internal combustion engine . . .'

'A past with transmat? Look how we arrived here.'

'The thing is – where's here?' asked Sarah.

They looked around them, baffled and confused. Only the middle of the area seemed relatively unchanged.

There was the sunken square, the fountain and the lions, the tall column with the figure on top.

'Well, at least Nelson's still on his column,' said Sarah.

'Is he?' said Tom grimly. 'Let's take a closer look.' He took her arm and they moved off. 'We'd better get away from this terminal anyway,' he said. 'Just in case our friend inside changes his mind about us.'

'Why didn't you just stop and explain?' asked Sarah. They crossed the road into the square and walked towards the central column.

'I wasn't sure it would be healthy. Didn't you recognise that cross in the transmat booth – and the man's uniform?'

'No. Did you?'

'You don't watch enough old war movies,' said Tom grimly.

They had reached the foot of the column by now and they stood staring upwards. The square was crowded and they noticed that people here looked a little different. There were fewer uniforms, for one thing, and a greater variety of civilian outfits. There were Japanese visitors too, all busily taking photographs of each other in front of the column.

Some things at least hadn't changed, thought Tom. Trafalgar Square was still a big tourist attraction. Only . . . there was something missing.

Trafalgar Square had always been famous for its flocks of pigeons, an attraction and a nuisance at one and the same time.

The progressively-minded complained about the health hazards, the mess and the little white blobs all over poor old Nelson. All over the visitors too, if they were unlucky. But generations of tourists, especially kids, had delighted in feeding the pigeons, and in being photographed with pigeons perched on their wrists or standing on their heads.

Recently the powerful Environmental Party had got the pigeons declared a protected species, so nobody dared touch them.

At least that's how it was in the Trafalgar Square they knew. But here . . .

'No pigeons!' said Tom suddenly.

They looked around. There wasn't a pigeon to be seen.

A sweet little white-haired old lady was standing nearby. She had overheard Tom's remark.

'Isn't it wonderful?' she said. 'One of the wretched birds soiled the Reichsminister's uniform, you know, at an official ceremony. The very next day he had the whole lot scientifically exterminated. Such an improvement!'

Tom and Sarah didn't reply. They reached the base of the towering column and stared upwards.

'Wait a minute,' whispered Sarah. 'That's not Nelson up there!'

The figure looked different somehow, though the column was so high it was hard to make out details.

Tom saw that the white-haired old lady was clutching an enormous pair of binoculars.

'Excuse me,' said Tom politely. 'Could we borrow your binoculars, just for a moment?'

The old lady looked a bit reluctant, but Tom gave her his most charming and boyish smile. 'Please?'

'Very well, but do take care of them.' She handed the binoculars over. 'They belonged to my late husband. He was in Unterseeboots, you know, before he became a Party official . . .'

She rattled on, but Tom wasn't really listening. He raised the powerful binoculars to his eyes, adjusted the focus and stared at the figure on the column. After a moment he passed the binoculars to Sarah.

'Take a look.'

Sarah raised the binoculars. She adjusted the focus and the figure on the column sprang into sharp relief.

She saw the statue of an oldish man in a plain civilian coat. So powerful were the binoculars that Sarah could see the statue's face quite clearly. The man had a little moustache, and a lock of hair falling over one of his eyes.

Sarah lowered the binoculars and looked at Tom.

'Funny-looking little chap, isn't it? And it's certainly not Nelson. Who is it?'

It was the old lady who answered, staring at Sarah in astonishment. 'Nelson came down off that column seventy years ago. Surely you must know that, my girl! That's our glorious leader up there, the first Fuehrer, who founded the Thousand Year Reich.'

Tom took the binoculars from Sarah and handed them back to the old lady. She looked suspiciously at him and said sharply, 'You know who it is, don't you, young man?'

'Oh yes, I know,' said Tom. 'It's Adolf Hitler.'

CHAPTER THREE

PARALLELS

'WHO?' SAID Sarah. 'I can't believe it . . .'

The old lady looked shocked.

Tom took Sarah's arm and led her away. They found an empty bench on the far side of the square and sat down.

From her bench the old lady eyed them suspiciously.

'Adolf Hitler,' Sarah repeated disbelievingly, as if in a daze. Then, as the history lessons – not her favourite – started to come back, 'German dictator . . . founder of the so-called National Socialist Party – Nazis, for short. Came to power in 1933, conquered most of the continent by the early forties. Defeated by England and America and their allies – when was it?'

'1945,' said Tom. 'He committed suicide.'

'That's right,' said Sarah. 'I remember now. So what's he doing lording it up on top of Nelson's Column?'

'I can only think of one possible explanation.'

'Which is?'

'Here – wherever here is – Hitler won!'

'I see,' said Sarah. She sat staring into space for a moment or two. Then she turned to Tom, her eyes bright with excitement. 'Of course . . . that's it!'

'What's what?'

'I know where we are. We didn't go forwards or backwards, we went sideways. We're in some kind of parallel universe!'

'Come again?'

'It's a theoretical concept,' said Sarah. 'At least, it used to be theoretical – now we've proved it! It's a great scientific discovery, Tom. We'll be famous!'

'Proved what? What is this theory anyway?'

'It explains certain interesting anomalies in particle physics,' said Sarah.

Tom gritted his teeth, trying to keep calm. 'It explains certain whats in what? Cut out the scientific gobble-degook. Keep it simple!'

'The theory is that everything that *can* happen *must* happen – somewhere. So if there's a world where this Hitler lost the war, there's one where he won.'

'And this is it?'

'Presumably. How else would it be Hitler up on that column instead of Nelson? Look at all these new buildings, the way the people are dressed, all the uniforms. This isn't our Trafalgar Square, Tom – it isn't our world, or even our universe.'

'Not our universe?'

'That's right. We're in England, in London, in Trafalgar Square – in a parallel universe!'

Tom stared at Sarah. He was astonished at how calmly she seemed to be taking things. Presumably she was so excited about proving this daft scientific theory that she hadn't realised the consequences for the two of them.

They were exiled, possibly trapped. Not just in a strange place but in an alien universe. How similar would it be to their own? And how different?

'How many of these universes are there anyway?' he asked.

'In theory an infinite number – one for every possible event.'

'And how come a malfunctioning transmat got us here?'

Now it was Sarah's turn to deliver the lecture.

'You know nobody's really sure how transmat actually works?'

Tom groaned. 'Now she tells me!'

'Well, one theory is that you go into another dimension, somewhere between the universes, then return to your own universe but in a different place. Well, we went into another dimension and returned to the wrong universe!'

'Sounds pretty mind-boggling to me,' said Tom, rubbing his aching forehead. 'On the other hand – here we are!'

'That's the problem, isn't it?' said Sarah. She was beginning to realise the full horror of their situation. She looked at Tom in sudden alarm. 'Here we are, so what do we do about it? How do we get back?'

'Maybe we should have stayed in that transmat booth and tried again. It might have worked properly, taken us back to our own universe.'

'Or to another, even worse one!'

'From what I remember about the Nazis, I don't think another one could be much worse. But we've got to do something . . .'

All kinds of thoughts were whirling through Tom's head.

If they couldn't get back to their own universe – and he had to admit it didn't seem very likely – what should they do?

Surrender themselves to the authorities? Nazi authorities?

Besides, who would believe them? They'd end up in prison. Or in a mental home . . .

Suddenly Tom shivered. Hadn't the Nazis believed in eliminating the unfit? They'd eliminated the pigeons.

He became aware that Sarah was looking at him in alarm.

'Tom, what is it?'

He decided not to share all his worrying thoughts. 'Look, Sarah, it's just possible we're jumping to conclusions. This parallel universe theory of yours is all very well, but there may be other explanations.'

'Name one!'

'I can't, not yet. We need a few more facts to go on.' He looked around. 'Not everything's changed, this part of London still seems to be a tourist area. The crowd seems to be pretty mixed.'

Sarah looked round as well. 'It's not that mixed.'

'What do you mean?'

'Look at the faces.'

Tom looked, and realised what she meant. He and Sarah had grown up in a racially mixed society. It was something they took for granted, like the transmat. And the transmat, of course, had broken down barriers even more.

In their universe people were black or white or brown or any of the many different shades in between. Apart from a few cranks, nobody thought much about it any more.

But not here.

There wasn't a single black or brown or coffee-coloured face to be seen – everyone was white. A surprising number were fair-haired and blue-eyed as well.

'There are those Japanese tourists,' said Sarah. 'But apart from them . . .'

'The Japanese were allies of the Nazis during the war,' said Tom. 'They probably have special status.'

'What about the rest?' demanded Sarah. 'Indians, West Indians, Africans, Chinese. What's become of them?'

Tom didn't reply. Mass deportations, perhaps, he thought. Racial purity was a vital part of Nazi beliefs. Or . . .

He looked up at the pigeonless sky and shuddered.

Suddenly a voice shouted, 'There they are! Hey, you two!'

They turned and saw three black-uniformed men hurrying across the square towards them. The one in the lead was the guard from the transmat booth. He must have realised that they looked different, that they had been bluffing, thought Tom, and decided to inform the authorities.

Instinctively Tom said, 'Come on, Sarah – run!'

They dashed across the square, crossed another main road and turned left, running past Charing Cross station, closed down now in their world but still busy in this one.

They heard shouts behind them, and the sound of running feet.

There was a long, narrow street beside the station and they turned right and ran into it. The street sloped downwards and Tom remembered that it led to the river. Maybe they could find somewhere to hide . . .

There was another station at the end of the street and beyond that the Embankment. Suddenly Tom realised that they'd run straight into a trap. Their pursuers were close behind them and the river formed a barrier across their path. They'd never reach a bridge without being spotted.

Sarah ran to the low stone wall and looked over it. 'Tom, look!' she called.

Tom ran to join her. A long string of barges was moored close to the bank.

Tom and Sarah looked at each other and nodded, their minds working as one. They climbed on to the Embankment wall and leaped into space.

The three SS guards pounded down the steep, narrow street and stopped, looking around them. The Embankment stretched away in either direction but their quarry was nowhere to be seen.

'I swear they turned down here,' gasped the transmat guard.

'Well, I didn't see them,' said another of the SS men. 'I reckon they ducked into the station. They'll be trying to get away.'

The three guards hurried back the way they had come.

Tom and Sarah crouched down between the bales and boxes on the deck of the barge.

'Now what?' whispered Sarah.

'We'll hide here for a bit until they've moved on.'

A shadow fell over them. They looked up and saw a huge, roughly-dressed man with a straggly beard.

'Clear off!' he roared. 'Lousy little river-rats! You'll find nothing worth stealing here. No food, all machinery.'

For a moment they just stared up at him in amazement.

'Clear off,' he said again. 'Or do I have to chuck you overboard myself?'

He advanced menacingly towards them.

'All right, all right, we'll go,' said Tom.

'And we're not thieves!' said Sarah indignantly.

'So what are you doing on my barge?'

'Hiding,' said Tom. 'They were after us.'

'Who was?' said another voice. 'Them SS swine?'

The second speaker was a scrawny little woman in a faded, shapeless dress. She came and stood beside the man.

Tom nodded. 'They chased us down to the river.'

'What have you done, then?'

'Nothing, really,' said Sarah. 'I think they just objected to the way we turned up here.'

'Look, if you've escaped from some work camp you can just clear off,' growled the man. 'It's a capital crime, helping escapers. High treason! I don't want to find myself under the axe.'

'They're not from no work camp,' said the woman. 'Look at their clothes. They're refugees, come over 'cause they've heard things are better over here.'

'Better!' said the man scornfully. He spat over the side. 'If things are any worse over there than they are here . . .'

'That's right, isn't it?' said the woman. 'You've smuggled yourselves across the Channel. Refugees, aren't you?'

'I suppose so,' said Sarah. 'We've come from a long way away.'

'Well, whoever you are you can't stay here,' said the man. 'You couldn't have picked a worse place to hide. All these barges are checked regular by the SS, in case we're smuggling. Just clear off, it'll be better for you, and a lot safer for us.'

'We've got to help them, Harry,' said the woman. 'For the sake of our own. You can see they're tired and hungry.'

'We can't help them. We daren't. We've got to move down to the City to unload soon, and they'll go over every barge.'

'At least we can hide them for a while,' the woman replied. 'Give them some food and some different clothes. They'll get picked up straight away looking like that.'

The man threw up his hands. 'All right, Nell, have it your own way, you always do! Let's get them out of sight.'

He led them along the deck of the big barge to an open hatchway and down some wooden steps into a stuffy little cabin.

Tom and Sarah sat on the edge of a bunk and Nell served them thick slices of coarse black bread spread with yellow grease, and strong sweet tea in chipped mugs.

'Substitute bread and substitute marge,' she said cheerfully. 'Real tea, though. My Harry gets it from a mate down the docks.'

She chattered on while they ate and drank, telling them about the hard life of the bargees, slowly ferrying goods up and down the country. It was a picture of hard work on low rations and low pay, constantly under the threat of a tyrannical authority.

'Whoever told you life was better over here had it all wrong,' said the man called Harry. 'We're kept stony-broke and ground down. Labour camp or the firing squad if you get out of line.'

'Half-starved as well,' said Nell. 'Nearly all the food is shipped back to New Berlin – and what's left goes to those devils in the SS.'

'I suppose they're all Germans,' said Tom.

'Some of them, yes, the high-ups,' said Nell. 'But there's plenty as English as I am.'

Harry looked at his watch. 'They'll have to go, Nell, we've got to move soon.'

Nell produced two bundles of clothing from a locker in the back of the cabin. 'Get out of those strange clothes and put these on so you won't stand out so much,' she said. 'They used to belong to our kids,' she added sadly, 'but they won't need them now.'

'What happened?' asked Sarah.

'They cheeked an SS inspector when he came on board,' said Harry gruffly. 'He arrested them on the spot and they got took off to a labour camp.'

'That was three years and we've heard nothing since,' said Nell. 'They'll have outgrown this stuff now – that's if they're still . . .' Her voice tailed off.

Tom and Sarah took turns to change at the back of the cabin.

Sarah found herself wearing a shapeless brown dress and a long coat. Tom got a jacket and trousers in some coarse grey material. Both wore thick-soled, heavy shoes.

'Well, off you go and good luck,' said Harry. 'I'd try and get out of London if I was you, you'll stand more of a chance in the country.'

'Goodbye,' said Sarah. 'Thanks for all the help.' Impulsively she gave Nell a hug.

A few minutes later Tom and Sarah were back on the Embankment, watching the string of barges chug away.

They turned and looked at each other.

'We look like a couple of tramps,' said Tom.

'I know,' said Sarah, 'but this is what everyone else is wearing. At least we'll blend in now – and we're so much better off than the people who used to own these clothes . . .'

Tom nodded silently.

'Now what?' asked Sarah suddenly.

'I'm less keen than ever to go to the authorities,' said Tom. 'I'd still like to find out more about what's happened here. What we need is a good history book. I wonder if they still have bookshops in Charing Cross Road?'

Sarah shrugged. 'Let's go and find out.'

Moving around the edge of Trafalgar Square – now called Adolf Hitler Place, a sign informed them – they made their way to Charing Cross Road – now Herman Goering Avenue. It had always been a street full of bookshops and that at least hadn't changed.

As they walked along the street Tom paused to look in a few shop windows. In his universe the different windows had been filled with books, tapes and CDs on every imaginable subject.

Here they were all very much the same. Against the background of the Nazi flag – a red background bearing a white circle filled with a black crooked cross – the same few titles appeared over and over again: *Adolf The Great – a Biography of our Beloved Leader;*

Heinrich Himmler – Architect of the SS State;

'Forward with the Fuehrer – Our Nazi Philosophy.'

Suddenly Tom spotted another title:

1940 – 2015
Seventy-five Glorious Years
Province Britannica and the Thousand Year Reich.

He pointed it out to Sarah. 'That's what we need!'

'Maybe we do, but I don't see how we can get it. I doubt if our Credcards will work here.'

'We could steal it, I suppose. I mean, it is an emergency . . .'

Sarah shook her head. 'We're in enough trouble as it is.'

She read a printed notice displayed beside the book. 'This says the book's published to go with a special exhibition at the London Reichsmuseum.'

'Presumably the good old British Museum,' said Tom. 'Which isn't all that far away. Come on!'

They hurried on up the road.

Halfway along they heard the sound of martial music. Everyone on the pavement came to a sudden halt. A parade of black-uniformed soldiers marched by, led by a small military band.

Tom studied them with keen interest. The marching men wore smart black uniforms with skull-and-crossbones badges – the infamous death's-head.

They were the SS, the crack storm troopers of the Reich. From Hitler's personal bodyguard they had grown into a massive private army, and from that into a separate state within the Nazi state.

Tom saw that, without exception, the marching soldiers were tall and broad-shouldered, with blond hair and blue eyes. They looked hard and tough and tremendously fit.

For some reason they gave Tom the shivers. They looked like robots, like clones, like something inhuman – or superhuman.

They were the Nazi killer elite.

The reaction to their appearance was extraordinary. Everyone came to attention, and those wearing hats took them off. Men and women alike raised their right hands in salute.

The soldiers strutted by and the crowd came to life again.

Tom and Sarah were about to go on their way when each felt a heavy hand come down and grip their shoulders painfully hard.

A harsh voice roared, 'You two! You're under arrest!'

CHAPTER FOUR

ACCUSED

THEY TURNED and saw a heavy, red-faced, middle-aged man in a brown uniform, his bulging belly straining against his belt.

He let go of their shoulders and glared down at them.

'Don't you know how to show proper respect when the SS go by?'

Suddenly Tom realised – they hadn't saluted.

'I'm sorry,' he said. 'This is our first visit to London. We were so impressed by the sight of the parade that we just froze.'

'We're on our way to see the exhibition at the Reichsmuseum,' said Sarah. ' "Seventy-five Glorious Years" – isn't it wonderful?'

Tom said humbly, 'You're a Brownshirt, aren't you, sir?'

'That's right.'

'I think the Brownshirts are wonderful as well. Don't you, Sarah?'

'Oh yes,' said Sarah eagerly. 'Just as wonderful as the SS!'

'They don't get the credit they deserve,' said Tom.

'We do our job,' said the Brownshirt gruffly. 'We may not be as glamorous as some, but we keep the streets safe.' He looked down at them. 'All right, be on your way. Don't forget to salute next time.'

He turned and strode away.

'You two were dead lucky,' said a voice beside them.

The speaker was a thin-faced, dark-haired young man. He wore a neat grey tunic suit and looked as if he might be a clerk in the civil service.

'Were we?' said Tom cautiously.

'Why?' asked Sarah.

'You were lucky it was a Brownshirt,' said the thin young man. 'Some of them are still almost human. If it had been one of the SS you'd be on your way to a work camp – sorry, a rehabilitation centre – by now.'

'Thanks,' said Sarah. 'We'll have to be more careful.'

'I would if I were you. Strangers to London, are you?'

'That's right,' said Tom. 'We've just arrived.'

'You'd better watch your step – this is the big city.'

He looked as if he expected a reply, but Tom just nodded. 'Thanks, we will.'

Tom and Sarah moved off, and the young man watched them go.

'What was he on about?' whispered Sarah as they hurried away. 'And what's all this SS and Brownshirts stuff?'

'The Nazis had several private armies, as well as the regular one. I think the Brownshirts were a sort of people's militia – a Home Guard, if you like. The SS were far more ruthless – and much more powerful.'

'Sounds like you've accepted my alternative universe theory.'

'I think I'll have to,' admitted Tom. 'It seems to be the only possible explanation. Let's take a look at this exhibition, anyway. The more we know about this universe the better – it'll help us decide what to do next.'

They made their way up Charing Cross Road – or rather, Herman Goering Avenue – and crossed New Oxford Street – now Heinrich Himmler Boulevard.

'Himmler!' said Tom when he saw the sign. 'He was the one who ended up running the SS. He was a weedy little nerd but a clever politician and a terrific organiser. The SS ended up in charge of pretty well everything.'

The British Museum was still in its usual place just behind New Oxford Street. It still looked like three temples stuck together in a row, and it was still surrounded by tall, black, gold-tipped railings. But now it was called the London Reichsmuseum, and its façade was draped with Nazi flags.

They crossed the road, dodging the still-unfamiliar traffic and went in through the narrow pedestrian gate. It was guarded by a massive SS storm trooper. They crossed the courtyard and joined the little crowd of tourists climbing the stone steps.

The foyer didn't seem to have changed much, although the whole place looked dusty and run-down. There was still the massive staircase leading upwards, guarded by two battered stone lions on huge square blocks. But now there was a rope barring the stairs and a printed notice, 'Upper Galleries Closed'.

They followed the signs to the exhibition, which took place in three long rooms just to the left of the main entrance.

'I think this used to be the bookshop,' whispered Sarah.

The notice outside the entrance read:

1940 – 2015
Seventy-five Glorious Years
Province Britannica and the
Thousand Year Reich

Fortunately admission appeared to be free.

The exhibition, when they reached it, was disappointingly primitive by the standards of their own universe. No holographic displays, no hand-held talking guides. Just a simple photographic presentation of a series of events, pinned down in black and white, with long explanatory captions underneath.

The captions and photographs were pinned along the walls, forming a long trail that was obviously meant to be followed.

Tom and Sarah joined the straggling line of tourists working their way dutifully round the exhibition.

The first photograph showed a group of disconsolate-looking, khaki-clad soldiers, arms raised in surrender.

The caption read, *1940 – German troops accept the surrender of the British Expeditionary Force, encircled at Dunkirk.*

'Aha!' said Tom.

Another set of photographs showed German troops landing on a beach. The caption read, *The beginning of Operation Sealion – victorious troops of the Reich make a successful landing near Dover.*

They trailed laboriously round the lengthy exhibition, looking at what seemed like hundreds of captioned photographs. There were so many that Sarah's head started to swim – she just couldn't take it all in.

Tom however was studying every photograph, every caption, with eager attention. Occasionally he muttered, 'Right!' or 'I see . . .' or 'So that's what happened!'

More photographs and captions told how the defeated Britain signed an armistice with Germany, and was absorbed into the Thousand Year Reich as Province Britannica.

One photograph did catch Sarah's attention.

It showed a small, dark woman and a slender, fair-haired man, robed and crowned and seated on twin thrones.

Sarah read the caption: *His Majesty King Edward the Eighth and Queen Wallis, restored to their rightful thrones by a benevolent Fuehrer.*

The memory of some old romantic story stirred in her mind.

'Wasn't he the one who gave up his throne because they wouldn't let him marry the woman he loved?'

Tom nodded. 'He was weak and selfish – and a German sympathiser from way back. When the Nazis won, Hitler must have put him back on the throne as a puppet king.'

Soon the black and white photographs were succeeded by others in colour. These showed the citizens of Province Britannica, leading happy and prosperous lives as part of the glorious Thousand Year Reich.

A whole series was devoted to the state funeral of Adolf Hitler in New Berlin.

'1986,' muttered Tom, studying the captions. 'He must have lived to be nearly a hundred!'

The exhibition went on and on, bragging about the achievements of the wonderful Thousand Year Reich. By now it seemed to include most of Europe, India, and large chunks of Africa as well.

Sarah noticed that in the African and Indian photographs all the people in the foreground were white, most of them in uniform. Indians and Africans appeared only in the background, usually as servants.

She pointed this out to Tom, who nodded. 'The Nazis must have taken over the British Empire,' he said. 'England gave its colonies independence after the war. Looks like the Nazis hung on to them.' He looked at Sarah. 'I've already found out most of what I want to know. Let's skip the rest and get some fresh air.'

They hurried past the rest of the exhibition – drawing shocked looks from their fellow tourists – and left the museum, sitting down on the top of the steps outside.

Tom sighed. 'Well, now we know!'

Sarah shook her head. 'How did such a horrible lot ever get into power in the first place?'

'Germany collapsed after the First World War,' said Tom. 'Inflation, mass unemployment, political unrest, the lot. Up popped the Nazis, a party of loony extremists, run by a collection of crooks, led by a mad, charismatic dictator.'

'Adolf Hitler.'

Tom nodded. 'Under Adolf the Nazis plunged the world into war, but in our universe they were totally defeated in 1945.'

'But not here . . .'

'Apparently not. In this universe the Nazis successfully invaded England. Maybe the Americans didn't even come into the war.' Tom's face was bleak. 'It's a tragedy, Sarah. History gone horribly wrong.'

Sarah found it hard to take in. She was a scientist, not

a historian, and it all seemed so long ago. She only knew Germany as a friendly, prosperous modern country. She was vaguely aware of this dark patch in its history, but it wasn't real to her, the way it was to Tom. She made an attempt to cheer him up.

'Come on, it can't be as bad as all that.'

'Oh can't it? The Nazis were – *are*, I suppose I should say here – totally evil. Racist, sexist, fascist, you name it. They believed in total state control. Forget democracy. There was only one party – them! No human rights, no civil liberties, no tolerance for minorities of any kind. Jews, gypsies, gays, even the handicapped and the mentally ill – they wanted them all wiped out. Anyone who opposed the state was imprisoned without trial, and tortured or murdered. They had all these horrible beliefs about Aryan purity and racial superiority.' Tom drew a deep breath. 'In our universe there are just a handful of loonies with ideas like that. With the Nazis, those ideas were official Government policy!'

Sarah found it hard to believe in the kind of society Tom was describing. But she was soon to see proof.

Suddenly she heard a voice shouting, 'There they are, officer. Sitting there!'

She looked up and saw a white-haired old lady coming out of the museum, a black-uniformed SS man beside her.

The old lady looked vaguely familiar.

'It's the old dear from Trafalgar Square, the one who

lent us the binoculars,' said Tom.

'I spotted them in Adolf Hitler Place,' the old lady was saying. 'The girl pretended not to know who our beloved Fuehrer was. She said he was a funny-looking little man! Some SS men came after them and they ran away. Later on I saw them again, in Herman Goering Avenue, and they didn't even salute the SS parade! Some slack fool of a Brownshirt let them off. He should have arrested them on the spot. I followed them here and they went round the exhibition making disgusting remarks about the Reich being defeated and the Fuehrer committing suicide. They're subversives, officer, traitors to the State! Arrest them!'

CHAPTER FIVE

HUNTED

TOM JUMPED to his feet, grabbing Sarah's hand and pulling her up after him.

'Run!' he yelled.

Sarah just couldn't believe that talking could be a crime.

'But we haven't done anything!' she protested.

'We know that but he doesn't. Run!'

'You two – stay where you are!' roared the SS man.

Tom and Sarah ran down the steps, dodging between the crowd of tourists coming in and out of the museum.

The SS policeman was so used to instant obedience that it took him a moment or two to realise he was being defied.

He drew his revolver.

'Shoot them!' screeched the sweet old lady. 'Shoot the filthy traitors down!'

Fortunately for Tom and Sarah the steps were crowded with terrified tourists. The SS man had every right to shoot down fleeing fugitives. But the Thousand Year Reich was trying to improve its image these days, and new directives had been issued.

This didn't mean that suspected criminals and traitors were treated any better. But beatings-up were supposed to be private rather than public these days, and killing innocent foreign tourists was definitely frowned upon.

The SS man raised his revolver and fired a warning shot in the air, hoping to frighten the fugitives into surrender.

The only result was to panic the crowd of tourists who began milling to and fro, screaming and shouting in terror.

The shot made Tom and Sarah run faster than ever, and they disappeared into the crowd.

Cursing, the SS man lumbered in pursuit of them, the frightened tourists scattering before him.

Tom and Sarah dashed down the steps, out of the museum gates and fled into the streets.

In the local SS command post everything was quiet. It usually was. London was a peaceful city these days. Ruthless policing combined with savage punishments kept it that way.

Beggars were instantly scooped up and sent to serve long sentences in labour camps. Muggers, burglars and drug peddlers were given a summary court-martial and shot the same day.

Such relatively petty crime was normally dealt with by patrolling Brownshirts. In the eyes of the SS, this was about all they were good for anyway.

To deal with major crimes, ones that endangered the Reich, SS command posts were scattered about the city.

They didn't have too much to do, apart from look sinister and terrifying and march in parades. All the same, the thought that squads of trained killers were on permanent stand-by helped to keep the population of London in order.

These days political protest was simply unheard of.

Lieutenant Niles, guard commander of Post Two, the SS post nearest the Reichsmuseum, was young and inexperienced, but he was fanatically keen.

His father, a millionaire industrialist, had given generously to Party funds. Niles was well aware that this had a great deal to do with his obtaining the coveted SS commission.

He was desperate to prove himself.

When the hotline telephone on his desk rang he snatched it up eagerly. 'Yes? What? Slow down and speak clearly, man, you're babbling.' He listened for a few minutes, making notes on a pad in front of him. 'Right, get back to your post and await further instructions.'

He slammed down the phone. 'Sergeant Wagner?'

A stocky, middle-aged man rose from his desk in the outer office and came unhurriedly into the room. 'Sir?'

'Emergency, sergeant. Subversive activity at the Reichsmuseum. Turn out the squad!'

Sergeant Wagner stared blankly at him. 'What exactly's happened, sir?'

Excitedly Lieutenant Niles relayed the SS policeman's story.

'The fool lost them in the crowd but they can't have got far. Take the squad and set up roadblocks round the museum. I'll alert the other guard posts. Hurry, man!'

The sergeant, a veteran of twenty years' service, didn't get excited very easily. He just stood there, frowning.

'Well, get a move on!' snapped Lieutenant Niles.

'With respect, sir – is it worth it? Turning out the other command posts for a couple of cheeky kids? We can tell the Brownshirt beat patrols to keep an eye out for them.'

Lieutenant Niles's answer came straight out of the SS training manual.

'Treason is like a plague, sergeant. One tiny germ can infect a whole city. I want these two found. We're the nearest squad to the scene, we ought to be the ones to catch them. Get on with it!'

'Sir!' said Sergeant Wagner woodenly. 'Description, sir?'

Lieutenant Niles scrabbled for his notes.

'One male, one female, both aged about fifteen, possibly older. The male is dark, the female fair.'

'Clothes, sir? Anything unusual?'

'No, just ordinary workers' clothing.'

'Not much to go on. City's full of young workers . . .'

'Then the sooner you get started the better. Move!'

'Sir!'

The sergeant hurried from the room, and Lieutenant Niles grabbed the telephone and dialled.

'Post Three? This is an emergency . . .'

As soon as he was reasonably certain they'd shaken off the immediate pursuit, Tom slowed down to a walk.

'Just stroll along,' he gasped. 'Try to blend in.'

Sarah nodded. 'Where are we making for?'

Tom looked around. They were walking along one of the smaller streets behind the museum.

'Search me,' he said. 'Just anywhere outside of the area.'

A thought struck him. 'Maybe we ought to try to get home.'

Tom's parents, Sarah's uncle and aunt, lived in a big old house in North London.

'Home?' said Sarah. 'How do we get there?'

'Walk, I suppose. It's not all that far. The streets seem to be much the same, even if they have changed all the names. At least we'd know where we were if we went home. We might even find someone who'd help us.'

Sarah said thoughtfully, 'You're assuming our home, our parents, our friends all exist in this universe?'

Tom shrugged. 'From what you say, it's a possibility, isn't it? We just don't know what's changed and what's still the same.'

'I'll tell you another possibility,' said Sarah slowly.

'What?'

'You just haven't thought it through, have you? If our family and friends do exist here, then maybe we do too!'

'Well, of course we exist . . .' Tom broke off, suddenly realising what Sarah was saying. 'You mean − other versions of us? Another Tom and another Sarah?'

'Why not? It's logical.'

Tom had a sudden picture of them both confronting their doubles.

He grinned. 'I always wondered what it would be like to be twins. Not sure I could cope with two of you, though.'

'It's no joke, Tom. It would be . . . weird.'

'I don't know,' said Tom. 'It'd just be a case of us helping ourselves − or do I mean the other way round? Anyway, it's worth a try, isn't it? Going home, I mean. What do you think?'

Sarah didn't reply. She pointed down to the end of the street.

A couple of black-uniformed men were setting a wooden barrier across the road. The gap in the middle was large enough for only one person. Slowing down, they watched as people went through the gap one by one. They were producing something, something the guards were checking before allowing them through.

'What's that they're showing the guards?' asked Sarah.

'Papers,' said Tom bitterly.

'What sort of papers?'

'Identity cards, passports, visas, travel permits. All the rage in totalitarian states.'

'You mean you're supposed to carry something with you just to prove who you are? That's terrible!'

Sarah was shocked at the very idea. Compulsory identity papers were completely unknown in her world, seen as an offence against everyone's civil rights. All she'd ever had to carry was her credcard.

'Anyway,' she went on, 'we haven't got anything like that to show them.'

'Wouldn't help if we had,' said Tom gloomily. 'That old bat who reported us will have given them our description.'

'So what do we do?'

'Cross the road – slowly – and look in a shop window on the other side. Then stroll back in the other direction.'

They did as Tom said, moving slowly and casually. Soon they were on the other side of the road, going back the way they had come.

There was a checkpoint at the end of that road as well.

They were trapped.

CHAPTER SIX

HIDEOUT

THEY CROSSED the road again and turned into a sidestreet.

When they turned out of it, into another, larger road there was another checkpoint at the end.

And so it went on. Every road led to another checkpoint, with black-uniformed figures checking people through.

'They've ringed the whole area,' said Sarah indignantly. 'It isn't as if we've actually done anything either.'

They ducked into another street and found themselves facing a set of familiar-looking black railings. They saw the curiously familiar shape of a big building.

'We're right back at the museum,' said Tom. 'We've worked our way round to the other side.'

'This part of it looks deserted,' said Sarah.

They walked over to the railings and stood looking up at them. They looked too high to climb – and anyway, there were those golden spikes.

'This is ridiculous!' said Sarah angrily. 'Look, why don't we go and give ourselves up? What can they charge us with anyway?'

'Showing disrespect to the Sacred Memory of the first Fuehrer,' said a voice.

They looked up and saw that a young man had suddenly appeared on the other side of the railings. He was thin-faced and dark-haired, and they'd seen him before. He'd spoken to them when they'd been stopped by the Brownshirt.

Tom looked hard at him. 'Sounds serious,' he said. 'What do you reckon we'll get?'

'Oh, five to seven in a labour camp . . .'

'Months?'

'Years.'

'But we haven't done anything wrong,' said Sarah indignantly. 'Not on purpose, anyway. We're just not guilty of anything!'

'Maybe not, but you will be,' said the young man calmly. 'Once you're arrested . . .'

'What do you mean?'

'Well, if you're arrested, you must be guilty of something, mustn't you? Otherwise the glorious Reich has made a mistake. And that just can't happen.'

'But if they can't prove anything . . .'

'They'll have your confession.'

'We haven't got anything to confess!' yelled Sarah.

'You'll think of something – once you've been in the hands of the SS for a few hours,' said the young man chillingly. 'Everybody confesses. Simplifies the process of justice no end.'

'Thanks for the advice,' said Tom. 'Looks as if we'd better get a move on.'

'I shouldn't bother,' said the young man. 'They'll have been tightening the cordon. You go back into any of these streets and you'll find a checkpoint at either end.'

'I see,' said Tom. 'What do you suggest we do, then?'

'You might consider joining me on the other side of these railings.'

'How?' asked Sarah.

The young man lifted something from under his coat and let it unroll down the railings.

It was a rope. He fastened his end to a couple of spikes and waved towards it.

Tom and Sarah hesitated.

'I'd get a move on if I were you,' he said. 'The offer is open for a limited period only . . .'

'Why should we trust you?' asked Sarah suspiciously.

'Well, if you'd sooner trust the SS . . .'

'He's right,' said Tom. 'We haven't any choice. Over you go, Sarah.'

Sarah grabbed the rope and hauled herself over the railings.

'Don't worry about the spikes,' said the man. 'This section has been specially blunted.'

He helped Sarah down the other side.

Tom took her place on the rope and climbed up after her. Like Sarah, he dropped down on the other side of the railings.

They watched as the young man pulled down his rope, coiled it up and stowed it under his coat.

'This way,' he said.

He led them between two deserted-looking buildings into a yard littered with builders' rubble.

'Abandoned improvements,' he said briefly.

He took them across the yard, moving aside a pile of crates to reveal a heavy iron door set into the wall of the building.

Producing a big, old-fashioned key, he unlocked the door and opened it, revealing a square of darkness.

Sarah and Tom went inside and the young man followed, locking the door behind them.

The Gauleiter of London Central District was paying a visit to Lieutenant Niles's SS command post.

For the lieutenant it was an unhappy experience.

The gauleiter sat at his ease behind Lieutenant Niles's desk.

The lieutenant was in front of the desk, standing rigidly to attention.

The gauleiter was a kind of local governor. He was also a general in the SS. He was a tall, elegantly handsome man, with a long, thin face and hard grey eyes. He had an acid tongue that could raise blisters on his terrified subordinates.

One of the few British-born members of the SS to achieve high rank, he was a man with powerful friends – and many enemies.

'Twenty-five checkpoints set up,' drawled the gauleiter. 'Over a hundred men deployed. This remarkable display of effort to pick up two youngsters babbling some kind of vaguely seditious nonsense. And to crown it all, you don't even find them!'

'I don't understand it, sir,' said Lieutenant Niles worriedly. 'We had the area sealed off within minutes. Every street was covered, every single person checked and interrogated. Yet there was no sign of them.'

'They were probably clear away before your first checkpoint was set up,' said the gauleiter dismissively. 'All these resources expended for nothing. You have shown a severe lack of judgement, Lieutenant Niles. Even if you'd caught them – which you didn't – I doubt if these young people would have been worth the effort. The resistance is a joke, and we all know it.'

'They were preaching sedition, sir!'

The gauleiter sighed wearily. 'I have read your notes concerning Mrs Winter's complaint, lieutenant. Are you aware of her background?'

'Background? No, sir. She appears quite reliable.'

'She is the widow of an important Party official. Her loyalty to the Reich is admirable, of course. However, since the death of her husband that loyalty has become somewhat – obsessive. The good lady sees treason everywhere. According to her local SS post, she denounces someone or other almost daily.'

'I'm sorry, sir. I had no way of knowing. I took her report at face value.'

'Her statement is extremely odd,' said the gauleiter. 'According to her, these young people were not addressing others or distributing leaflets. They were talking quietly to each other about some kind of – alternative history.'

'A history in which the first Fuehrer had lost the war,' said Niles in shocked tones. A third-generation British Nazi, fanatically loyal, Niles had been born under the rule of the victorious Reich. Indoctrinated with Nazi ethics since birth, he believed in them totally.

'Some kind of childish fantasy,' said the gauleiter. 'The very concept is totally absurd. Foolish, certainly, but not necessarily criminal. They are reaching puberty, lieutenant. I have adolescent children myself, and I can assure you that it is a difficult age . . .'

The lieutenant said nothing, and the gauleiter rose. 'I take it Mrs Winter will be coming in to make a full and formal deposition?'

'She has an appointment tomorrow afternoon, sir.'

'See if you can get any more details out of her. Try to

get a more accurate description. Show her our suspect files.'

'Very good, sir,' said Niles gloomily.

The gauleiter smiled. 'Don't take things so hard, lieutenant. Too much zeal is better than too little.'

He nodded and strode out.

Lieutenant Niles resumed his rightful place behind his desk, quietly seething at the injustice of the gauleiter's words.

Opposition only made his convictions stronger.

He was quite sure now that this mysterious young couple were dangerous traitors and he was equally convinced that they hadn't had time to avoid his cordon.

So where were they? If they hadn't got away, then they were still somewhere in the area. And if they were still in the area, then he could still find them.

That would show that sarcastic swine of a gauleiter.

Lieutenant Niles sat with his chin in his hands, thinking hard . . .

Tom and Sarah followed the thin young man along a maze of gloomy stone corridors lined with rusty metal pipes, up and down staircases, along more corridors.

The corridors were shrouded in darkness, with only the occasional dim light burning here or there.

Finally he led them into a big, cellar-like room and switched on a light. The place was furnished with an assortment of battered furniture, some of it fairly modern-looking, some incredibly ancient.

An electric kettle, a tin tray and a mismatched assortment of crockery stood on a corner table.

He waved an arm around the room. 'It's not much, but it's home. Sit down and I'll make some tea.'

Tom and Sarah sat down on a sagging sofa while he plugged in the ancient electric kettle.

Soon they were all clutching mugs of strong, hot tea.

Tom sank back wearily. 'Thanks, that's a life-saver. I hadn't realised it was so tiring being hunted.'

Sarah looked round. 'Where are we?'

'In the bowels of the Reichsmuseum,' said the young man. 'What you might call the maintenance area. There are all kinds of passages and corridors, all interconnected. It's safe enough, for the moment. Most of the museum is closed down now – they only use it for the odd meeting or exhibition.'

'Why's that?' asked Sarah.

It was absurd, she thought. They were hiding in the depths of a derelict museum, hunted by human monsters which belonged in the past, and making polite conversation as if they were at a vicarage tea party.

'Why's the museum closed?' The young man took a swig of tea. 'Simple – there's almost nothing left to exhibit. Nearly everything was shipped off to New Berlin in the forties and fifties. It's in the Fuehrer Museum now, or the Goering Collection.' He looked from one to the other of them. 'Now the civilities are over, I think it's time for some explanations.'

Tom and Sarah looked at each other.

'Sorry,' said Tom. 'We'd better be on our way. Thanks for the help – and the tea.'

The young man reached inside his coat and produced a huge, old-fashioned revolver.

'I want some answers from you two,' he said. 'And they'd better be convincing – or you won't be leaving here at all.'

CHAPTER SEVEN

SUSPICION

SARAH LOOKED at the revolver with a kind of indignant amazement.

'Don't be so ridiculous,' she said scornfully. 'What's the point of helping us to escape and then threatening to shoot us?'

'I didn't rescue you for your sake but for ours,' said the thin young man with equal scorn. 'I simply wanted to get you off the street. You two are a menace.'

'Why?' demanded Sarah. 'Who to?'

The young man didn't answer.

'I can tell you that,' said Tom. 'He's obviously involved with some kind of resistance movement.'

The young man gave him a suspicious glare. 'Am I? What makes you so sure?'

'You said "ours". Besides, there's always a resistance movement in a repressive society like this. History's full of them.' With deliberate provocation Tom added, 'Few of them are much use. Half-baked intellectuals, students . . . they seldom achieve anything.'

'Oh, don't they?' said the young man angrily. 'Well, let me tell you, we're nearly . . .' He broke off and laughed. 'Very neat, I nearly fell for that one. On second thoughts, I don't think I'll tell you anything. I'm still waiting for some answers from you.'

'Why did you say we were a menace?' persisted Sarah.

'Oh, do try and think,' said the young man. 'Suppose your friend here's right, and there is a resistance movement? The only way it could hope to survive is by absolute secrecy.'

'So?'

'So we don't need idiots like you two wandering the streets spouting treason at the tops of your voices. Look at the size of that SS operation you stirred up. It's only by pure luck that none of our people got caught up in it.'

Tom and Sarah looked guiltily at each other.

'We're sorry,' said Tom. 'Really we are. It wasn't intentional, was it, Sarah?'

'Of course not! We'd no idea there was going to be all that fuss.'

'Which brings me back to my original question,' said the young man. 'Who are you?'

Tom said, 'My name's Tom – Tom Martin.'

Sarah said, 'I'm Sarah Martin.'

'Brother and sister?'

'Cousins,' said Tom. 'What's your name, by the way?'

'Why do you want to know?'

'Why not? We have to call you something.'

'You can call me Mark,' said the young man. 'All right, so much for names. Now, where do you come from?'

Tom and Sarah looked at each other and then back at the young man.

'This is the difficult bit,' said Tom.

Mark was growing visibly impatient. He waved the revolver.

'For the last time, will you answer me?'

'Oh, we'll answer,' said Sarah hastily. 'We'll tell you everything, the complete and absolute truth.'

'The trouble is,' said Tom, 'you're not going to believe us.'

Lieutenant Niles of the SS sat brooding at his desk. The gauleiter's mocking tones, his sardonic remarks about errors of judgement echoed in Niles's mind, making him writhe with embarrassment at the memory.

Niles was still convinced that the two young traitors couldn't have escaped his dragnet.

So logically, if they hadn't got away, they were still there somewhere, in the area, hiding . . .

But where?

The answer, Niles suddenly realised, was obvious.

He raised his voice. 'Sergeant!'

The sergeant appeared from the outer office. 'Sir?'

'I want all the men you can raise, sergeant, and the vehicles to carry them. We're going on a raid.'

'Yes, sir. Where to, sir?'

'We're going to raid the Reichsmuseum . . .'

'So there you are,' said Sarah.

'I told you that you wouldn't believe us,' said Tom.

Mark looked at him with a mixture of scorn and admiration. 'You're completely mad. But at least you're creatively mad.'

'It may seem mad to you,' said Sarah. 'But I can tell you, it seems even madder to us!'

Mark shook his head despairingly. 'Even if I accept this parallel universe nonsense – which I don't – your version of history doesn't make sense. How could the Fuehrer manage to lose with all the advantages on his side?'

'It was a near thing,' admitted Tom. 'Hitler was beaten by bad luck and some bad decisions.'

'Oh no he wasn't,' said Mark bitterly. 'The Nazis invaded England in 1940. Japan made a peace treaty with America, and the Americans stayed neutral. The Reich has ruled over Europe, England included, for seventy-five years.'

'In your universe, but not in ours,' said Sarah.

Mark laughed. 'A parallel universe – one where the Fuehrer lost! I wonder what it would be like.'

'We can tell you exactly what it's like,' said Sarah. 'We've lived in it all our lives.'

'Go on then, tell me,' said Mark unexpectedly.

'You mean you believe us?'

'No, of course I don't. I just want to see how far you've worked out this delusion. What happened in your universe after the war?'

Sarah looked at Tom. 'You're the history student – you tell him!'

Tom gave Mark a potted history of the last seventy-five years – his and Sarah's seventy-five years.

He told of the surrender of the Japanese – after they'd suffered the effects of two atomic bombs.

He told of the Cold War between England and America and communist Russia that followed.

'Things were pretty bad for a while,' said Tom. 'A lot of people were afraid there'd be a full-scale atomic war, that the whole planet might be destroyed.'

Mark was listening with a sort of unwilling fascination. 'It sounds as if you were in even worse trouble than we are! What happened?'

'Things got better,' said Tom simply. 'Russian communism collapsed, the Cold War fizzled out . . .'

'And now I suppose you live in a wonderful world full of sweetness and light?' sneered Mark.

Tom shook his head. 'Of course not. There are all kinds of problems. But everybody's trying.'

'The invention of transmat made a big difference,' said Sarah. 'It's hard to hate foreigners when you can step into a transmat booth and be in their country in a matter of seconds – or they can be in yours.' She looked enquiringly at Mark. 'Didn't transmat have any effect here? I know you've got it, because that's how we arrived.'

'Transmat's only for Nazi Party officials,' said Mark. 'Ordinary people never get near a transmat booth.'

Tom nodded. 'I suppose that's only logical. You can't run a repressive dictatorship if everyone can go anywhere they like whenever they feel like it.'

Sarah turned to Mark. 'Go on, then,' she said. 'It's your turn.'

Mark stared at her. 'What do you mean?'

'Tell us what happened in your universe . . .'

CHAPTER EIGHT

SPIES

MARK THOUGHT for a moment.

'Not very much,' he said gloomily. 'The Reich doesn't approve of change.'

'Wasn't there any resistance – after the invasion, I mean?' asked Tom.

'There was, at first, but it was ruthlessly stamped out. The SS moved in and took over everything – government, education, business, industry. Once they'd got rid of what they called the "alien elements" and wiped out all the rebels they started trying to win over the rest of the population. If you opposed the SS you got crushed, but if you stayed in line you were treated pretty well. Eventually the people of New Britannica were given full rights as citizens of the Reich. We can vote – only for Party candidates, of course. We can even join the SS.'

Sarah looked horrified. 'Do English people really do that?'

'Of course. If you're going to get anywhere at all in life you've *got* to join the SS.'

'What about on the continent?' asked Tom. 'Do they treat the other occupied countries the same way?'

'Things are much worse there than they are here. For some reason Britain gets special treatment.'

'Hitler always admired the British,' said Tom. 'He said Britain and Germany were natural allies, and ought to join together to run the rest of the world!'

'Lots of British people have risen quite high in the SS,' said Mark. 'We not only live under the Nazi regime, we help to run it! Most of our rulers here in England are English now – though the very top jobs still go to the Germans.'

'How could people just go along with all this?' asked Sarah.

Mark shrugged. 'Our parents were nearly all born under the regime – and my generation have never known anything else.'

Tom said, 'But it's your generation that's starting to rebel?'

Mark nodded. 'I suppose our parents were still stunned by the defeat of *their* parents. They just accepted things – they felt they were lucky to have survived. We've had time to think, to realise things ought to be different.'

'What are you trying to do?' asked Sarah.

Mark shrugged. 'Eventually to overthrow the regime,

ridiculous as it seems. But it will take time – generations, maybe . . .'

'Maybe we can help,' said Sarah. 'If we're stuck here, we may as well do something useful.'

'What could you do?'

'We could tell people about the way the world ought to be,' said Tom. 'The way it still can be, if you can get rid of this lot. In our universe the Thousand Year Reich lasted just twelve years – and that was far too long! You've had seventy-five years of it already.'

'If people would listen . . .' whispered Mark. He broke off, shaking his head. 'I've just realised what I'm doing!'

Sarah frowned. 'What do you mean?'

'I'm talking to you as if you were sane! As if all this parallel universe nonsense were really true.'

'It *is* true,' said Sarah fiercely. 'And we are sane, don't pretend you can't see it. Don't start backsliding now!'

Mark rubbed a hand across his eyes. 'You're certainly convincing, I'll say that! But then, lunatics are supposed to be convincing, aren't they?'

'Knock off this lunatic business,' said Tom indignantly. 'You've seen enough of us now to know we're no more mad than you are.'

'That's right,' said Sarah. 'And why would we tell you a story like this if it wasn't true? What could we hope to gain by it?'

'You could be spies, trying to find out more about us.'

'With a ridiculous story like this?' said Tom. 'If we were spies we'd say we were – I don't know – fellow rebels, escaped from prison or something. And we'd have a good story, and all the clothes and papers to back it up.'

'Don't you see?' insisted Sarah. 'It's the fact that our story is so unbelievable that makes it so convincing.'

Mark laughed. 'There's something not quite right about the logic of that, but I can't seem to work out what it is!'

'So what are you going to do about us?' asked Tom.

'I'm not sure. I think I'll have to leave that up to the meeting.'

'What meeting?' asked Sarah.

'There's a meeting of my resistance cell here, in about half an hour. People should start arriving before long. If the meeting agrees we'll pass you up the line, and let someone higher in the organisation deal with you.'

'And if the meeting doesn't agree?' asked Tom.

Mark glanced down at the revolver in his hand. 'Let's hope for your sake they do! Meanwhile, how about another cup of tea? I'll make some fresh.'

Pocketing the revolver, he went over to the table.

Tom and Sarah exchanged glances. Sarah nodded towards Mark, who was busy with the kettle. Tom looked back and shrugged. As so often happened, he found he could almost read Sarah's mind.

Should they try to jump Mark and escape?

Tom considered. Even if they succeeded without getting shot – which was by no means certain – where would they go? They'd just be on the run from the resistance and the SS. Mark was the only halfway friendly contact they had in this strange universe.

Better to stick with him.

Tom shook his head slightly and wiggled his outstretched hand in a wait-and-see gesture.

Sarah nodded, showing that she understood and agreed.

They watched while Mark made fresh tea and carried it over to them on the tin tray.

Suddenly the door was flung open. A thin, dark-haired girl appeared in the doorway. She looked very like Mark, and Sarah guessed she was probably his sister.

Mark swung round, the tray still in his hands. 'Annis! You're early. I thought you were at . . .'

'I came to warn you,' said the girl. 'The meeting's been cancelled. We've had a tip-off – there's an SS squad on its way here.'

'What? But why . . . ?'

'I imagine they're looking for us,' said the girl. 'They'll be here soon, and they'll start searching the building. It'll take them a while to find this place, but we'd better get away before . . .' She broke off, looking at Tom and Sarah.

'Who the devil are these two?'

'They're on the run from the SS,' said Mark. 'I

thought I'd better take them in.'

The girl looked hard at them, staring into their faces, first Tom's and then Sarah's.

'You're the one who's been taken in,' she said. 'I recognise these two. They're not on the run from the SS, they're *in* the SS!'

Tom and Sarah both jumped up. 'That's rubbish!' said Sarah. 'I've never seen you before in my life!'

'We couldn't possibly be in the SS, anyway,' said Tom. 'We've only just – arrived here.'

'And they don't even *have* an SS where we come from,' said Sarah.

The girl gave them both a look of pure hatred.

'You may not know me, but I recognise you. If you want to work undercover you should try to keep your faces out of the Party propaganda papers.' She turned to Mark. 'Where did you find these two, anyway?'

'They were talking out of turn in the street. Somebody reported them and the SS set up a big dragnet. I thought I'd better get them out of the way.'

'You always were a trusting fool,' said the girl. 'Don't you see? It was all a trap. They knew we were somewhere in the area so they dressed these two up as refugees and sent them out as bait. And you fell for it! I expect they kept them under observation to see where you took them. Or maybe they managed to send out some sort of signal.'

'Not while I was with them,' protested Mark.

'How do you know? They're probably wearing homing devices so the SS can keep track of them.'

'Look, this is all nonsense,' said Tom. 'We're not SS spies, and we only want to help you.'

'They told me this incredible story,' said Mark. 'About a different universe, one where the Nazis had been defeated and the world is free.'

He sounded, thought Tom, as if he didn't want to stop believing in the idea.

The girl wasn't impressed. 'Trust you to fall for some fairy story. Look, we've got to get out of here.'

'What about these two?'

'You've got your revolver, haven't you?'

'Yes, of course, but . . .'

'Then kill them,' said the girl. 'Kill them both now!'

CHAPTER NINE

THE RAID

MARK LOOKED horrified. 'We can't just murder them in cold blood.'

'I can if you can't,' said the girl fiercely. 'Here, give me the gun and I'll do it for you!'

It was quite obvious that she was perfectly serious.

A line from an old poem flashed through Tom's mind. Something about the female of the species being more deadly than the male . . .

He suddenly realised that ever since the girl had come in, Mark had been standing there with the tin tray in his hands.

He glanced at Sarah and raised his eyebrows. Sarah gave the briefest of nods. As always, they were on the same wavelength . . .

As Mark moved to put down the tray, Tom gave it a tremendous kick from underneath. There was a tinny crash and tray, teapot and cups shot high in the air.

Tom grabbed the astonished Mark and shoved him hard, sending him sprawling on to the old sofa.

Sarah grabbed the girl and pushed her into Mark, who was struggling to get up. The two collapsed in a tangle of arms and legs.

By now Tom had the door open. He and Sarah dashed out into the corridor, slamming the door behind them.

As they ran along the dimly-lit corridor they heard an incredibly loud bang, and something whistled between them.

Instinctively Tom glanced round.

The girl was standing by the open door of the room they'd just left, the big revolver held outstretched before her in two hands.

There was another bang, and then Sarah grabbed his hand and yanked him around the corner.

They ran on . . .

It was just getting dark as a terrified nightwatchman swung open the main gate of the Reichsmuseum.

The SS truck drove into the courtyard of the museum and screeched to a halt at the bottom of the steps.

A squad of black-uniformed SS storm troopers clutching Schmeisser submachine-guns piled out of the back. Lieutenant Niles and Sergeant Wagner descended in a more dignified manner from the front.

Sergeant Wagner formed up the squad in three ranks and Lieutenant Niles addressed them. He was a great believer in keeping the men informed. He believed it kept up their morale.

'We turned out earlier hunting a couple of subversives, men. Unfortunately we weren't successful. Tonight we will be. I'm pretty sure they didn't get past us. They doubled back and hid in here. Now we're going to hunt them down like the treasonable rats they are.'

Sergeant Wagner looked dubiously at the looming bulk of the museum.

'Pretty big building, sir,' he said quietly. 'And with respect, we're not even sure there's anyone in there . . .'

Ignoring him, Lieutenant Niles turned to the night-watchman, a shivering, white-haired old man in a drab brown overall.

'You – what's your name?'

'Herrick, lieutenant. May I ask what this is all about, sir? I was ordered to open up for an SS squad but that was all. I know the museum well, perhaps I can help? If I knew what you were looking for . . .'

'We believe that some enemies of the Reich have taken refuge in the building.'

Old Herrick felt a stab of fear. He'd been connected with the resistance for some time. It was at his suggestion that they'd used the basement rooms for a hideout. The resistance could never have made use of the museum without Herrick's knowledge – and his help. Fortunately this keen young lieutenant seemed to be too dim to realise that. Herrick decided to go on playing the doddering old imbecile. It was his only hope . . .

'I suppose it's possible, lieutenant,' he quavered. 'They could have got in before closing time and hidden. There are so few of us left on the staff now . . .'

'Wherever they are, we intend to find them. Come along, you!'

The old nightwatchman led them up the steps to an open door.

When the squad was assembled Lieutenant Niles looked around. The cavernous foyer itself was dimly lit, and the big staircase on the left led upwards into pitch darkness.

Lieutenant Niles pointed. 'Can't we get some light up there?'

Old Herrick shook his head. 'Most of the museum has been permanently shut down for years. The electrical systems have broken down, sir, and they've never been repaired.'

Sergeant Wagner said, 'There are torches in the truck, sir.'

'Then get them in here.'

Wagner nodded to a corporal who scurried out to the truck, returning with an armful of torches.

'Right, sergeant,' said Lieutenant Niles. 'Form the men into small groups, one torch to each squad.'

Wagner barked out orders and the sub-groups were formed.

When the process was complete Niles snapped, 'Right, let's go! And remember, these people are enemies of the Reich . . .'

He was interrupted by shots, first one, then another. Muffled but recognisable, they came from somewhere inside the building.

Lieutenant Niles shot Sergeant Wagner a glance of triumph. 'Hear that? They're in here all right!'

'Why are they shooting at each other?' demanded Sergeant Wagner logically.

Lieutenant Niles was too excited to worry about petty details. 'Who cares? Maybe they're fighting amongst themselves.' He turned back to the squad. 'You all heard those shots. These people are armed and dangerous. Shoot them on sight!'

Lieutenant Niles and Sergeant Wagner led the way up the huge stone staircase, past the two massive stone blocks and the crouched, battered stone lions – in the gloom they looked poised to spring.

The SS men clattered up the stone steps. Halfway up the staircase divided into two smaller stairways to the left and the right, which curved round to meet at the top.

The SS squad found themselves in a high-ceilinged, cavernous room, bare except for a few mostly empty glass cases.

Lieutenant Niles swept his torch round and suddenly found himself looking at a grinning skull. He recoiled for a moment, before realising that the skull was part of an ancient human skeleton, stretched out in a long glass case. It was one of the relatively few museum exhibits that the Reich hadn't bothered to ship back to Berlin.

Niles shone his torch around the room, revealing big doorways to the left and the right, leading to other rooms.

He had been intending to lead the first patrol, to be the first one to find and shoot down the subversives.

But there was something very unpleasant about the thought of those darkened and empty galleries. Room upon room – and who knew what enemies might be lurking in there . . .

And, after all, it was an officer's job to direct, to remain in command. He decided upon a change of plan.

'Off you go, men! Spread out and search the different galleries,' he ordered. 'And remember, these people are armed and dangerous. Shoot on sight, and shoot to kill. The sergeant and I will stay here and guard the staircase. Get moving!'

One by one the groups moved away, leaving Niles and Wagner waiting behind in the gloom.

Lieutenant Niles glanced towards the skeleton, and hurriedly looked away. He had a nasty feeling it was grinning at him.

Sergeant Wagner cleared his throat. 'They may not be up here at all, sir.'

'What do you mean, sergeant?'

'Well, this place must have a big basement area – boiler rooms, storerooms, service corridors, that sort of thing. They might be holed up down there.'

'I'm aware of that, sergeant,' said Niles stiffly.

He'd overlooked that possibility completely, and he had an uneasy suspicion that Wagner knew it only too well. 'First things first,' he went on. 'We'll check out this area and then go down and search the basement. If they're not up here, they must be down there.'

'Yes, sir.'

Privately, Sergeant Wagner thought this whole enterprise was useless. You'd need an army to search a place this size.

This was what happened when you gave people officer's commissions in the SS because their families had political influence.

Something else was worrying him even more.

'Excuse me, sir.'

'What is it now, sergeant?'

'I think we ought to go on the patrol with the lads, sir. They're not long out of training and they haven't had combat experience. There's a chance they'll panic.'

'SS men do not panic, sergeant,' said Niles loftily. 'We shall remain here to coordinate the operation.'

We'll remain here because you haven't got the guts to stay with the men, thought Sergeant Wagner. Leading from behind, sonny, that's your style.

Twenty years of military discipline stopped him from expressing the thought out loud.

He tried again. 'Let me go in with them, sir.'

But Lieutenant Niles didn't fancy waiting alone in the dark.

'I need you here with me, sergeant.'

Sergeant Wagner had a bad feeling about this operation. It was ill-conceived and badly organised, and all his instincts told him it would end in disaster.

Still, he told himself, he'd survived a lot of dim officers in his time and he hoped to survive many more.

Sergeant and officer stood waiting in the darkness.

CHAPTER TEN

ESCAPE

TOM AND Sarah were running along a series of gloomy corridors. Sarah led the way, and Tom was quite happy to leave it to her. Sarah had an uncanny sense of direction. He knew from their holidays together that she never seemed to get lost and could always find her way back to wherever they'd started.

She paused at a junction and hesitated.

'Where do you think we are?' asked Tom.

'I think we're somewhere near the front entrance. We came in round the side and as far as I can tell . . . This way – I think!' She chose a corridor and they hurried along it.

'Do you think they're still after us?' she asked.

'I doubt it,' said Tom. 'I can't hear any footsteps behind us, and they'll be worried about getting away themselves.'

'What was all that stuff about recognising us? About our being in the SS?'

'Well, you're the one who thought of it,' said Tom.

'Thought of what?'

'Our having other selves . . .'

Sarah wasn't paying attention. She stopped. 'Listen! I can hear voices.'

They could hear shouted orders and the clatter of booted feet coming from somewhere ahead.

'Shall we turn back?' whispered Sarah.

Tom shook his head. 'We could wander around in these corridors for ever. Let's creep a bit nearer. Maybe we can find a way out.'

They moved cautiously down the corridor, which ended in a flight of steps. The steps led them up into a long room lined with dusty lockers. The room led into a smaller one with a wooden table, some chairs and a desk.

'Staff quarters,' whispered Tom.

On the other side of the room there was an open door. Through the door came the sound of many footsteps.

They moved quietly across the room and slipped out of the door.

They found themselves in the main foyer of the museum, behind one of the big stone blocks that flanked the staircase.

Peering around the stone block they saw the last of what sounded like a large group of black-uniformed SS men clattering up the stairs.

Tom and Sarah looked further into the foyer. It was

empty – and the main door was standing open.

They looked at each other and both nodded.

They were about to make a dash for it when someone came round the edge of the stone block and stopped short, staring at them in utter amazement.

Mark and his sister Annis were slipping silently through the darkened galleries. Convinced that the two strangers had betrayed them, Annis had refused to use their usual way in and out. They were making for another secret exit on the far side of the building.

Annis moved into another gallery and found herself caught in the beam of a torch. Instantly she threw herself down and the blast of submachine-gun fire tore over her head, smashing an empty glass case.

A voice yelled, 'This way! They're over there!'

There was the sound of running feet and suddenly more torch beams flashed around the gallery and more submachine-guns roared in the darkness.

Mark slipped behind an unsuspecting SS man and curved an arm round his throat, bearing him to the ground. Seconds later Mark rose with the man's submachine-gun in his hands.

He sprayed bullets at the advancing torches, putting out several, and then threw himself down as the blast of counter-fire roared over his head.

He felt someone touch his arm. It was Annis.

'Come on,' she whispered.

Keeping low, they crawled quickly from the gallery and fled back the way they had come.

Behind them the battle raged on.

Tom and Sarah found themselves facing a white-haired old man in a brown overall. He stared at them in amazement.

'What are you two doing up here? Don't you know this place is crawling with SS?'

'We're on the run from the SS,' said Sarah. 'Please, can you help us?'

The old man peered at her through the gloom. 'I thought you were . . . ?' he broke off. 'Never mind.'

Tom pointed to the open front door. 'Can we get out that way?'

'It'll be risky. They've left a man outside with the truck. If he sees you, he'll shoot. I could try to hide you until they leave.'

'I'm not sure they're going to leave,' said Tom. 'If this lot don't find us they'll send for reinforcements and go over the whole place.'

Suddenly a rattle of gunfire came from upstairs. There were shouts and yells, and then more gunfire.

An armed SS man ran up the steps and into the foyer.

Tom and Sarah ducked back into the shadows and the old man moved forward.

'What's going on?' demanded the SS man.

Shouts and the sound of gunfire were still echoing from the floor above.

'Sounds like they've run into trouble,' said the old man. 'I think I heard someone calling for help.'

The SS man hesitated for a moment and then ran up the stairs.

'Right,' said Tom, as he disappeared from view. 'Now's our chance.'

He and Sarah ran across the foyer and slipped out of the door. They paused briefly in the darkness at the top of the steps and looked around.

Parked in the open square just in front of them was a black SS truck, the cabin door wide open.

'Come on,' said Sarah. 'Let's run for it.'

'Run be blowed,' said Tom. 'This is too good a chance to miss!'

He ran over to the truck and climbed up behind the wheel, waving Sarah to the passenger seat beside him.

She ran round to the other side. 'What do you think you're doing?'

Tom grinned. 'I always told you my weird hobbies would come in useful!'

As Sarah scrambled into the passenger seat he started the truck and put it into gear. The truck lurched into motion, heading for the still-open main gate.

CHAPTER ELEVEN

GUNFIGHT

FACE WHITE, eyes staring wildly, Lieutenant Niles came clattering down the steps.

'Phone!' he screamed. 'Quickly, man. I need some reinforcements, there's a whole gang of armed terrorists up there . . .'

Suddenly he broke off, listening.

The sound of an engine starting up came clearly through the open door.

'That's the truck,' said Niles incredulously. 'Our truck!'

He ran to the door. He was just in time to see the SS truck move jerkily across the courtyard and vanish through the main gate.

In his panic, Niles ran down the steps and actually started to chase the truck. Then, realising his folly, he turned and ran back into the museum. 'Phone!' he screamed again. 'They've stolen the truck!'

Upstairs in the darkened galleries, the gunfight was still raging. Torch beams swept wildly through the darkness and the muzzle flashes of the Schmeissers flamed repeatedly.

Sergeant Wagner moved cautiously towards the fighting, edging his way round the side of the room. He went through one gallery after another, until he saw the muzzle flash of a Schmeisser.

He stopped, raising his voice in a parade-ground bellow. 'This is Sergeant Wagner. Cease fire! That's an order, do you hear me? Cease fire!'

Gradually the rattle of gunfire stopped.

'Hold your fire!' repeated Wagner. 'And stand still! Everyone stand absolutely still!'

He switched on his torch and swept it around the room.

The beam revealed a scene of carnage and devastation, with bullet marks on the walls and shattered glass from broken display cases everywhere.

It revealed tense-faced storm troopers aiming their submachine-guns.

It showed men slumped against the walls, clutching bleeding wounds.

And it showed six motionless forms sprawled on the floor in pools of blood.

Of Lieutenant Niles's gang of armed terrorists there was no sign.

Wagner moved to the nearest body and knelt beside it, checking for a pulse. He did the same to the others and then stood up.

'Dead, all six of them,' he said briefly.

'It was the terrorists, sarge,' said one of the men.

'We didn't stand a chance,' sobbed another. 'They were waiting for us!'

'It was an ambush,' someone shouted from the darkness. 'That cowardly swine Niles sent us straight into a terrorist ambush!'

'Terrorists be damned,' said Wagner bleakly. 'Those six men were killed by machine-gun fire – our own machine-guns.' He looked round the stunned and silent group. 'You know what you've been doing, you damned fools? You've been fighting each other!'

On the far side of the building Mark and Annis climbed out of an open ground-floor window into a darkened yard.

They crossed it, climbed over a wall, dropped into a quiet sidestreet and hurried away.

'We'd better get well away from here,' said Annis. 'The SS will move an army in soon, search every corner.'

'We'd best stay out of Central District altogether,' said Mark grimly.

'What about Herrick? Do you think he'll be OK?'

'I hope so,' said Mark. 'He'll do his doddering old idiot act, it'll probably fool them.'

'What about all our plans?' asked Annis. 'Will all this delay things?'

Mark considered. 'I shouldn't think so. We won't be able to use the museum any more but there are other places. I don't think this is more than a minor setback. Whoever those two were, they didn't find out much. As soon as we're safe I'll get a message to the Leader.'

'How?'

'Never you mind!'

'It's a bit frustrating working for someone you don't even know,' grumbled Annis.

'It's better that way,' said Mark. 'What you don't know they can't beat out of you.'

'Do you know who he is?' asked Annis curiously.

'What makes you so sure it's a he?' teased Mark. 'Could be a she for all you know – or all I know, come to that.'

'You really don't know who the Leader is either?'

'Don't know and don't want to,' said Mark. 'All I know is that he – or she – unified all the different resistance groups and got us working together. And there's a plan. There'll be an important meeting soon. Maybe we'll see the Leader then.'

They hurried on their way.

The stolen SS truck roared through the night, with Tom clinging grimly to the wheel. Driving on real roads in a place where they still had traffic was very different from driving in an internal combustion rally on a private road or an abandoned airfield.

They'd nearly had a crash at the very beginning when Tom discovered that everyone else was driving on the wrong side of the road.

It was Sarah who pointed out that the British seemed to be driving on the right now. No doubt the tidy-minded Reich had brought them into line with the rest of Europe.

In Tom and Sarah's universe, the British still clung to their obstinate left-handedness.

Fortunately everyone seemed happy to keep out of their way. Nobody wanted any trouble with an SS truck.

'Doesn't seem to be much traffic,' said Sarah as they jolted along.

'Just as well with my driving,' said Tom. 'I expect cars are a luxury, reserved for bigwigs.' He gripped the wheel tighter as they bounced over a pothole.

'They don't take very much care of the roads here,' he grumbled. 'Half the streetlights aren't working either!'

'Mind if I ask where we're making for?' asked Sarah.

'Home!' said Tom briefly. 'That was the original plan, wasn't it?'

'We just drive this thing up the street and park outside our front door?'

'Hardly! We drive it as far as we dare and then dump it somewhere.'

'And what do we do when we get home?' demanded

Sarah. 'Knock on the door and say, "Look, we know you've already got one Tom and Sarah, but how would you like another set?"'

'I don't know what we do or say when we get there,' said Tom. 'It all depends on how things are. But if our parents are still the same people, even in this universe, maybe they'll help us.'

'Or maybe they'll be dedicated Nazis and turn us in!'

'We just don't know, do we?' said Tom. 'But with the SS *and* the resistance movement after us now, we've got to find someone to help us!'

The truck sped on.

'Aren't you going too fast?' asked Sarah.

'Probably,' said Tom grimly. 'But they'll be chasing us soon, and setting up cordons ahead. I'd like to get as far as I can before we have to abandon the truck . . .'

Sergeant Wagner had assembled the squad – six dead, nine wounded and the rest unharmed – in the foyer. He and the corporal were tending to the more seriously wounded with field dressings.

Sergeant Wagner was doing his best to salvage a disaster. He knew heads were going to roll over the night's events. He only hoped that his wouldn't be one of them.

Old Herrick had produced an antiquated first-aid kit and was caring for the minor wounded. He told himself that even a wounded SS man was still a human being. He hadn't quite convinced himself, but he was trying.

Lieutenant Niles stood looking on, struggling to regain his self-control. He knew that the operation had gone disastrously wrong, and he was desperately preparing his excuses.

There was a roar of vehicles from outside. Niles went to the door and saw a convoy drawing into the yard. It was led by two ambulances. Behind them came six trucks, followed by a shiny black Mercedes-Benz staff car.

Stretcher-bearing medics jumped out of the ambulances, ran up the steps and whisked away the wounded.

SS storm troopers jumped out of the trucks and formed squads. They carried submachine-guns, and they were equipped with field radios and portable searchlights.

Some of the storm trooper squads spread out and surrounded the perimeter of the museum buildings.

The others flooded into the museum and disappeared up the stairs. Convinced by Lieutenant Niles's panicky call that there was a real emergency, the SS was reacting with its accustomed efficiency. This was a special assault team and, unlike Niles's unfortunate patrol, they were seasoned combat veterans.

Nobody paid the slightest attention to Lieutenant Niles.

When everything was underway a tall SS captain jumped out of the front passenger seat of the staff car. He opened the rear passenger door, stepped back and saluted.

The Gauleiter of London Central District got slowly out of the car. His uniform was immaculate and his jackboots gleamed.

Returning the captain's salute he walked unhurriedly up the steps. He went into the foyer, looked round and then crooked a finger at Lieutenant Niles.

Niles hurried over to him and saluted.

The gauleiter looked him over for a moment.

'Well, lieutenant,' he said gently. 'You really do seem to have surpassed yourself. Would you care to give me your account of tonight's events?'

The bored Brownshirt patrolman stood at the crossroads, watching the truck come down the long, straight road towards him. It was being driven, he thought, dangerously quickly.

He stepped forward, ready to stop the truck.

As it drew closer he recognised the SS markings and hesitated. The Brownshirts had no real authority over the SS.

All the same, the truck was being driven far too quickly . . .

The Brownshirt grinned. It would be a real treat to arrest an SS man for dangerous driving.

There was no love lost between the two organisations.

The Brownshirts thought the SS were a bunch of arrogant and snobbish thugs.

The SS scorned the Brownshirts as amateurs, working-class yobs and part-time soldiers.

The Brownshirt stepped into the road and held up his hand.

The truck didn't stop. It swung around him in a wide curve that took it on and off the pavement and went on its way.

The Brownshirt jumped back, cursing. He stood staring after the truck in astonishment. When the truck had swung round him he'd got a brief glimpse of the driver and passenger.

They didn't look like any SS people he'd ever seen.

He turned and ran back towards his command post.

CHAPTER TWELVE

CRASH

TOM STEPPED on the accelerator and the truck lurched forward even faster.

'That was a near one. Do you think he spotted us?'

'I'd be amazed if he didn't,' said Sarah. 'You practically ran over him.'

'I was doing my best *not* to run over him,' said Tom indignantly.

'Hadn't we better ditch the truck?'

'Soon,' said Tom. 'When we lose the truck we start walking – and we're still quite a way from home . . .'

The truck sped on its way.

'Now let me see if I've got this straight,' said the gauleiter gently. 'You decided, on no evidence whatsoever, that the two teenage subversives you failed to find earlier today were hiding somewhere in this museum.'

'But they were, sir,' said Lieutenant Niles eagerly.

The gauleiter held up a black-gloved hand and Niles subsided.

'So you take a squad of SS men, work them up into a patriotic frenzy and send them – *send*, not *lead*, lieutenant – into a series of pitch-black galleries, equipped with Schmeisser submachine-guns and one or two torches, whereupon they promptly panic and start shooting one another.'

Sergeant Wagner crashed to attention. 'Sir!'

The gauleiter raised an eyebrow. 'Yes, sergeant?'

'With respect, sir, there were terrorists – one terrorist, at least. We heard shots when we first arrived, and one of the wounded men had been shot with a heavy calibre pistol.'

'One terrorist,' repeated the gauleiter. 'And the attempt – the unsuccessful attempt – to capture this one terrorist has cost us six dead storm troopers, nine more wounded, and an SS truck. You're lucky there weren't one or two more of them, they'd have wiped out the whole damned squad!'

There was no answer to this, and Sergeant Wagner didn't attempt to make one.

The gauleiter turned back to the unfortunate Niles.

'There'll have to be an official enquiry into this incident, lieutenant. Quite frankly, you'll be lucky to come out of this with your commission. What your father will say, I shudder to think.'

Niles's father was an old friend of the gauleiter.

It didn't help.

White-faced and trembling, Lieutenant Niles was too frightened to reply.

The gauleiter sighed and turned away. 'Captain Miller!'

The tall SS captain was talking to the operator of a field radio. He listened for a moment and then came hurrying over.

'Sir?'

'Any results yet, captain?'

'Nothing here at the museum, sir, not so far. They've already checked most of the galleries. The perimeter team haven't found anything either. But there's a report on the stolen truck. A Brownshirt patrolman saw it heading towards North London. Being driven very fast, he said, nearly ran him over.'

Niles was so excited that he overcame his fear.

'Did he see who was driving?'

'Somebody quite young apparently, not in uniform. He had a girl with him.'

Niles turned excitedly to the gauleiter. 'It's them, sir, the ones who started all this. The ones we missed this afternoon, the ones who were hiding here. The description fits exactly.'

'One young male and one young female?' said the

gauleiter. 'Not exactly precise, is it?'

'I'm sure it's them, sir,' persisted Niles.

'Perhaps,' said the gauleiter sceptically. 'We'll soon know, I imagine. I take it steps are being taken to apprehend this vehicle, captain?'

'The roadblocks are going up now, sir.'

'Good. Let me know as soon as you hear anything.'

'It's time to ditch the truck, Tom,' urged Sarah. 'That Brownshirt is bound to have reported us. Besides, we're pretty close to home now.'

'Right,' agreed Tom. 'I'll turn down the next quiet sidestreet and we'll abandon it . . .'

But it was already too late. Tom turned a corner and found himself heading straight towards an SS roadblock. Heavy wooden trestles were blocking the road ahead, and armed storm troopers were manning the barrier.

Luckily the road was pretty wide at this point. Tom swung the wheel hard and the truck made a screeching U-turn. Seconds later they were hurtling back the way they had come.

But it was all for nothing. As they went back round the corner they saw black-uniformed figures shoving trestles across the road.

'What are you going to do?' asked Sarah steadily.

'There's still a gap in the middle − if I can squeeze through . . .'

Tom aimed the truck at the rapidly-closing gap and stamped on the accelerator. Sweeping the trestles aside, the truck smashed through the barricade and roared on.

'Well done!' shouted Sarah. 'The only trouble is, we're heading straight back to central London.'

'Not for long,' said Tom grimly. 'They'll be putting a cordon round the area but they can't block *every* road . . .'

He turned left and left again, and soon they were heading north once more.

'They doubled back in front of one roadblock and crashed through another,' reported Captain Miller.

The gauleiter stroked his chin.

'How very enterprising! Do we have any idea where they are now?'

'They were last seen heading back in this direction, sir.'

'They'll have doubled back again by now,' said the gauleiter positively. 'Something tells me they're determined on heading north. Step up the barricades and send out extra patrols. I'd like them taken alive.' He yawned. 'Well, I'm going home. Captain Miller, stay here and supervise the search. I doubt if you'll find anything now, but it has to be done. Sergeant Wagner, you will stay here and assist the captain.'

'Sir!'

'I am satisfied you did your best in difficult circumstances, sergeant. Carry on.'

'Sir.'

'Lieutenant Niles, as the officer in command you must bear responsibility for this fiasco. As I said, there will have to be an enquiry. Until then you will carry on with your normal duties. Try not to get in any more trouble.'

Niles nodded miserably, but didn't speak.

The gauleiter strolled over to the museum doorway.

'Our fugitives seem to be making for my part of the world. Perhaps I'll run into them on the way home!'

Jokes made by senior officers are always funny, and Captain Miller laughed dutifully. 'I'm sure you'll be able to deal with them, sir.'

The gauleiter nodded, and went down the short flight of steps to his staff car. His driver leaped out to open the door for him, and the gauleiter got in the back, relaxing on to the soft leather upholstery.

The driver got into the front seat and the staff car glided away.

It was the third roadblock that did for them.

Tom was driving along a steeply curving, narrow road bordering a section of open heath. His plan was to ditch the truck as soon as he could find a suitable spot.

They were pretty close to their home now, and Tom still held to his vague plan of asking his parents for help – his alternative universe parents. Perhaps it wasn't a very good plan, but it was all he could think of . . .

Suddenly he saw the roadblock at the top of the hill.

The hill was too steep and the road too narrow to turn.

Tom did the only thing he could. He swung the truck sharply to the right and headed into the blackness.

The truck smashed through some trees and skidded down a steep and muddy slope.

It overturned, throwing them both across the cab, and everything went black . . .

CHAPTER THIRTEEN

CAPTURE

THE GAULEITER of London Central District leaned back in his comfortable seat as the staff car glided through dark London streets.

There wasn't much of a nightlife in London under the Thousand Year Reich. Late nights and noisy celebrations were discouraged. Most public establishments were closed by ten p.m.

There was an official curfew at midnight.

Respectable citizens were well-advised to be home in bed before then. Anyone found on the streets had better have official permission, papers and permits, and a good reason for being out and about.

The gauleiter's eyes were half-closed and he might have been half-asleep. In fact, he was wide awake, and his mind was racing.

The affairs of Province Britannica were at a critical

stage, and there was much to occupy his mind.

A great deal depended on the events of the next few days.

He found himself curiously troubled by this strange business at the museum. It seemed to make no sense.

Who were these young people who courted arrest by criticising the Reich in public?

Nobody brought up in Province Britannica, no citizen of the Reich anywhere in the world, would dare to do such a thing.

Where did they come from – some other planet?

He remembered the account of the old woman who had first reported them. She said they been talking about another world – or was it another universe?

A universe in which the first Fuehrer had lost, and the Thousand Year Reich had fizzled out after a dozen years . . .

Madness.

Then there was the resistance angle. The gauleiter had made it his business to know a great deal about the struggling resistance movement, and this didn't fit any known pattern of activity . . .

The gauleiter sighed.

Whatever it all meant, things had been made much worse by Lieutenant Niles's catastrophic mishandling of the situation. SS storm troopers shooting each other down could cause a major scandal in the Party. It was the sort of thing that provoked awkward questions from New Berlin – the last thing he wanted right now.

It would all have to be hushed up, the gauleiter decided.

The Niles enquiry could be held in secret – on security grounds. To avoid scandal, Niles would escape being cashiered, much as he deserved it.

A formal reprimand and a transfer to the Siberian Frontier would have to meet the case . . .

The gauleiter's mind drifted back to the two mysterious young fugitives. The boy dark, the girl fair – the descriptions could fit anyone.

His musings were interrupted by the crackle of the staff car's radio. He slid back the partition and leaned forward.

'What is it?'

'Message from Central, sir. Patrols have located the missing truck in North London, just on the edge of the heath. The terrorists have crashed the truck and fled on to the heath on foot. The patrols are confident of rounding them up very shortly.'

The gauleiter considered for a moment, and found his curiosity too strong to resist.

'Get the location and take us there – it can't be far out of the way.' He smiled. 'This whole business has given me a great deal of trouble. I'd like to be in at the finish!'

Tom became aware that someone was shaking his shoulder.

A familiar voice called, 'Tom, wake up!'

Tom groaned. This was a familiar experience. Sarah was an early riser, he liked to lie in. She was always hauling him out of bed to go off on some daft expedition somewhere.

Where were they right now? At home? On holiday? He seemed to remember some kind of nightmare, an alternative universe full of sinister, black-uniformed Nazis chasing after them . . .

'Tom, wake up, will you?'

Tom opened his eyes to discover that it hadn't been a nightmare after all.

He was lying on a patch of damp grass next to an overturned truck, and a dishevelled-looking Sarah was kneeling beside him, trying to wake him up.

'All right, all right,' he groaned. He struggled to sit up and winced as a stab of pain shot through his head.

Sarah was looking anxiously at him. 'Are you all right?'

Tom put a hand to his head and winced as his fingers found a tender bump on his forehead.

'I think so, more or less. You?'

'I'm fine, thanks to you. You broke my fall.'

With a little help from Sarah, Tom got to his feet. He looked round. 'How did we get out here?'

'I heaved you out of the cab. I thought it might blow up or something. Can you walk?'

'I suppose so. Where to?'

'We'd better get away from here. They're coming after us.'

Tom could hear distant – not very distant – shouts, and the sound of men crashing through the bushes.

'Right, come on, then. If we can lose them on the heath we may still be able to reach home . . .'

The staff car drew up beside a little group of SS men standing beside a road barrier. One of them, an enormous corporal, was talking into a field telephone.

He sprang to attention as the gauleiter got out of his car. 'This is a great honour, sir . . .'

'Have you got them?'

'Any minute now, sir. The foot patrols have got them surrounded at a place called the Vale of Health.' He laughed. 'Won't be too healthy for them!'

'Take me there,' ordered the gauleiter. 'And get this barrier moved. Since our fugitives are on foot, it's hardly needed any more, is it?'

The SS men sprang to obey and the corporal led the gauleiter away down the hill.

Very soon they came to a narrow side road which led into a steep natural hollow on the edge of the heath. A road ran down into the hollow and there was a scattering of houses. Suddenly two running figures, a boy and a girl, appeared between the houses.

More running figures, black-clad SS men, appeared behind them.

'We've got them bottled up now, sir,' said the corporal. He drew his revolver.

The gauleiter drew his own revolver and fired in the air.

Down in the hollow, hunted and hunters froze.

'Don't shoot!' shouted the gauleiter. 'Nobody is to shoot. I want them taken alive.'

When he saw the two SS men barring the road out of the Vale of Health, Tom knew it was all over.

Perhaps there was still a chance – for somebody.

'I'll keep them busy, Sarah,' he gasped. 'See if you can dodge past, there are only two of them.'

Summoning the last of his strength, Tom dashed headlong up the slope and hurled himself at the largest of the two SS men.

The man raised an enormous fist and clubbed him down.

Everything went black for the second time . . .

Someone was shaking his shoulder, and a familiar voice was calling, 'Tom, Tom, wake up!'

Tom groaned. Hadn't this all happened before?

'Tom!' said the voice again.

It wasn't Sarah this time though; it was a man's voice, even more familiar.

Perhaps he really was home in bed this time and the Nazis were just part of a horrible dream.

But they weren't . . .

Tom opened his eyes and found he was stretched out on a wet, cobbled street. Directly in front of his eyes were a pair of gleaming jackboots.

With an effort he raised his eyes and saw a tall, immaculately-uniformed SS officer looking down at him.

The officer had dark hair, thick black eyebrows and lean, cynical features.

It was a face Tom knew well – a face very like his own.

'Dad!' he gasped – and slid down into blackness for the third time that night.

Later that evening, in his flat in a luxury block reserved for SS officers, Lieutenant Niles was reluctantly putting away his uniform.

Jackboots, black trousers, black tunic with cuff-badges, peaked cap – all were brushed and folded and stowed reverently away in the big wardrobe, ready for the next day.

In drab civilian slacks and shirt, Peter Niles looked at his reflection in disgust. If he wasn't an SS officer he was nothing.

Somehow he had to redeem himself.

It was all the fault of those two mysterious fugitives.

At the museum they'd led him into disaster.

To make things worse, he couldn't even discover what had happened to them.

There was a rumour that they'd been captured.

Then another one that there had actually been two sets of young people, two subversives and two innocent victims kidnapped by the resistance.

Then a security blackout had descended on the whole thing and nobody was allowed to talk about it any more.

Somehow Niles knew, just knew, that if only he could discover the truth about them he would be vindicated, a hero.

Brooding and obsessive, he sat planning his next move.

CHAPTER FOURTEEN

HOMECOMING

WHEN TOM recovered consciousness he was in a proper bed, between clean, white sheets. What's more, nobody was urging him to wake up. It was, he thought, a definite improvement.

He snuggled down between the sheets, emerging slowly and reluctantly from sleep.

Perhaps this time it really was all a dream.

He opened his eyes and saw that he seemed to be sleeping in a kind of tent.

After a moment he realised – he was in a four-poster.

Wherever he was, he definitely wasn't at home.

Somebody drew back the four-poster curtains at the end of the bed, and then the curtains at the bedroom window, letting in bright, summer sunshine.

Squinting through half-closed eyes, Tom saw that he was in an incredibly large room, furnished in an elaborate, old-fashioned style. Through the window he saw green lawns stretching away in the distance, with a view of a lake and a handsome white bridge.

The whole view had an elegant, formal air – an eighteenth-century air. The view, like the bedroom, gave Tom the feeling that he was in some kind of stately home.

Still, at least he was in the best bedroom, not locked up in the cellar. Had something else extraordinary happened? Had he somehow slipped back in time?

Tom looked at the girl who was opening the curtains. She wore a simple, overall-type, dark-blue dress – it looked modern enough.

It looked like some kind of maid's uniform.

The girl saw Tom looking at her and did a sort of bob – she was actually curtseying! What's more, she looked frightened.

Frightened of him.

'Forgive me, excellency, I didn't realise you were awake,' she said hurriedly. 'I'll bring your breakfast at once, and I'll inform your mother.'

Tom simply stared at her, too astonished to speak.

She curtseyed again and hurried away.

Tom sat up in bed and looked down at himself. He was wearing white pyjamas – white silk pyjamas. They fitted perfectly and felt comfortable, even luxurious, but they certainly weren't his.

They went with the four-poster, the big, elaborate bedroom and the fancy view.

Tom leaned back against the pillows, thinking hard.

After a moment the door opened and the girl came back with a laden tray. She put it on a table beside the bed and fussed around him, fixing up a sort of wooden bridge to put the tray on, so that he could sit up in bed and eat in comfort.

There was orange juice, coffee and scrambled eggs, bacon, mushrooms and toast, all under a series of silver dishes.

Tom suddenly realised that he was ravenous. He couldn't remember when he'd last had a proper meal – it must have been in another universe.

He polished off everything on the tray, while the maid looked on anxiously.

'Is everything satisfactory, excellency?' she asked.

'Everything's fine – and cut out the excellency stuff.'

The girl looked terrified. 'It is the proper form of address, excellency,' she said and set about clearing away the tray.

As she left the room, a plump, brown-haired woman came in. She saw Tom sitting up and rushed across to him, enfolding him in a suffocating hug.

'Tom! You're better! Oh, I'm so glad. I've been so worried about you!'

Gently Tom disengaged himself. 'It's all right, Mum,

I'm fine, don't fuss!'

He sat back and looked at her. It was his mother, of course, and yet – it wasn't. It couldn't be.

Any more than an SS officer could be his dad.

Thoughtfully Tom studied his new and different mother – Mum, mark II. She was the same – yet different.

The most obvious difference was her size. Tom's mum, his real mum, hated the thought of putting on weight. She fought the flab with twice-weekly visits to a gym and kept a careful eye on her diet. This woman was what you might call comfortably plump.

Then there was the hair. Tom's real mother was a not-quite natural blonde. This version had brown hair with streaks of grey.

Lastly there were the clothes.

Tom's mother was an executive with a big financial corporation, and she was always smartly and fashionably dressed, usually in some kind of business suit.

This woman wore a long velvet dress, comfortably loose and curiously old-fashioned looking.

For some reason, a German word popped into Tom's mind.

Hausfrau.

What was that phrase the Nazis were so fond of, the one defining a woman's place in the world?

The three Ks: *Kirche, Kinder, Küche.*

Church, Children, Kitchen.

This woman looked as if she'd settled happily for all three. Sarah wasn't going to like it in this society.

'Is Sarah all right?' he asked.

'Sarah's fine, she's been up for ages. Shall I ask her to come and see you?'

'No, that's all right, I'll get up now.'

Immediately she started to fuss.

'Do you think you should? The doctor said you had a mild concussion, you need plenty of rest . . .'

'I said I'll get up,' said Tom firmly.

She gave way at once – definitely not like his real mum.

'Very well, dear, I'll get the maid to bring you some clean clothes, the ones you arrived in were in a terrible state.'

She put her hands on his shoulders and said anxiously, 'You still haven't told me what happened to you. We were expecting you to come back from New Berlin tonight or tomorrow – and then your father brought you back yesterday evening all bruised and battered. What happened?'

Tom leaned back on the pillows and groaned artistically. 'I'm sorry, I just can't seem to remember. It's all so confused . . .'

'It must be the concussion. Never mind, your father will explain everything when he gets back this evening. Are you sure you're well enough to get up, dear?'

'Yes!' said Tom, making a quick recovery. 'Right now,

please! Can I have my clothes?'

'I'll see to it at once, dear.'

She hurried from the room.

Half an hour later, Tom was up and dressed. He was wearing shirt, slacks and a tunic-style jacket, all made from some soft grey material, all fitting perfectly.

He came down an elegant staircase, through a foyer and out on to a paved terrace where he found Sarah admiring the view.

It was the same one he'd seen from his bedroom window, rolling lawns sweeping down to a little lake.

She rushed up to him and gave him a quick hug. 'Tom, are you OK?'

'I'm fine. Baffled but fine. I like the outfit.'

Sarah was wearing a blue velvet dress, not unlike the one worn by his alternative-universe mother.

'Dead stylish, isn't it? I haven't worn a dress for years. I asked for some slacks and they looked horrified. It seems women don't wear the trousers around here.'

'They certainly don't. Have you met the new model Mum?'

Sarah nodded. 'New model aunt, in my case.' She looked at Tom and said cautiously, 'She seems – very nice.'

'Nice but dim,' said Tom cheerfully. 'I shudder to think what the original would say if she could see her other self.'

He took a quick look round. There was a maid – there

seemed to be an endless supply of them – at the other end of the terrace, but she was well out of earshot.

'Do you know what's going on, Sarah?' he continued. 'Why are we being treated like VIPs?'

Sarah shrugged. 'I assume we've been mistaken for the genuine articles – the Tom and Sarah who exist in this universe.'

'Mum – I suppose I'll have to call her Mum – said something about them being expected back from New Berlin.'

'Let's hope they take their time . . .'

Tom had a sudden idea. 'Maybe they won't turn up at all.'

'What do you mean?'

'Maybe we all got switched. Maybe they're wandering around in our world, as confused as we are.' He looked round at the big country house. 'I keep thinking there's something familiar about this place.'

'Of course there is,' said Sarah. 'Don't you know where you are? This is Kenwood – Kenwood House.'

In their universe Kenwood House was an eighteenth-century mansion on Hampstead Heath, carefully preserved and open to the public.

Tom looked around in astonishment. 'So it is! We came here for a picnic once. What on earth are we doing here?'

'We live here,' said Sarah calmly. 'It goes with your

father's job. A man of his importance can't live just anywhere.'

'Don't be daft. Dad's just a university lecturer . . .' Tom broke off, remembering the SS officer he'd seen last night. 'But things are different here, aren't they?'

'I'll say,' said Sarah. 'In this universe, Kenwood House is the official residence of a top SS official. His Excellency, the Gauleiter of London Central District – in other words, your dad!'

CHAPTER FIFTEEN

HIGH LIFE

TOM KNEW that what Sarah was telling him was true.

He'd known ever since last night when he'd seen that tall, black-uniformed figure gazing anxiously down at him.

He'd pushed it to the back of his mind, something he was unwilling to deal with before he absolutely had to.

'Here, you'd better come and sit down,' said Sarah. She led him to a little table on the terrace.

'Want some coffee or tea?' she asked.

Tom sat down. 'Do you think they'd have Coke?'

'I imagine they have everything,' said Sarah. She raised a hand and one of the maids came scurrying over.

She curtseyed. 'Excellencies?'

'Have you got any Coke?'

The girl gave Tom a terrified look. 'Your excellency?'

'Soft drink,' said Tom. 'Cola. Anything will do.'

'I think so,' said the girl breathlessly. 'I'm almost sure. I'll just go and see . . .'

She hurried away as if her life depended on it.

'Why are they all so scared?' asked Tom. 'Don't tell me Mum beats them or something, she hasn't changed that much.'

'I was talking to some of them earlier,' said Sarah. 'They're not quite so frightened of me. I suppose it must be because I'm only a girl!'

'So what did they tell you?'

'They're volunteer-workers from the other Nazi provinces, France and Holland and places like that.'

Tom nodded. 'I suppose they treat them all right. Pay and holidays and all that sort of thing?'

'They don't get paid and they don't get holidays.'

'What? Why do they stand for it?'

'They're glad to do it,' said Sarah. 'And as you can see, they're very keen to please.'

'What happens if they don't please? Do they get shot or something?'

'Oh no,' said Sarah. 'They just get sent back. From the way they talked it sounds like the worst thing that could possibly happen to anybody.'

The girl hurried back, carrying a tray. On it were two Cokes in the classic fluted bottles, two crystal glasses, a bowl of ice.

She put down the tray and curtseyed.

'Is that satisfactory, excellencies? It was all I could find, I do hope it's what you wanted.'

'That's perfect,' said Tom. 'Thanks a lot.'

The maid hurried off and Tom and Sarah poured their drinks.

Sarah looked at the bottle. 'Imported from America.'

She looked around, taking in the stately home, the terrace, the hovering servants. 'Talk about living the high life!'

'Nothing's too good for the SS – and their families,' said Tom sourly. He paused for a moment, and took a sip of Coke. 'You remember when we were talking to that chap, Mark, in the museum? You were horrified at the idea of English people joining the SS.'

Sarah nodded.

'Well, just look who Dad turns out to be!'

'I can imagine how you feel.'

'Can you? He's not your father . . .'

'He's my uncle and as good as a father to me,' said Sarah.

'There you are then,' said Tom. 'You know Dad as well as I do. I'm not saying he's perfect; he's got a sharp tongue and a bit of a temper at times. But his heart's in the right place about things that really matter. He *hates* cruelty and injustice and racism and everything this rotten regime stands for.

'How can he be a part of it, like this? Not just a part, but a top SS bigwig!'

'All right, calm down,' said Sarah. 'You're not being entirely fair.'

'What do you mean, fair? There's no possible excuse . . .'

'Your father's in his forties, right?'

'Forty-five,' said Tom. 'He married late.'

'So he was born in, what, 1970. In this universe the Nazis had already been in power in England for thirty years! It was all he'd ever known. He just made the best career for himself he could in the only world he knew.'

'There's some kind of a resistance movement, isn't there? We've met some of them. He could have joined that!'

'He's got a wife and child to worry about,' said Sarah. 'Not to mention a niece.'

'I suppose so,' said Tom gloomily. 'I don't think I like this universe, Sarah. It's turned my mum into a happy cabbage and my dad into Erich von Stroheim!'

'Who?'

'Famous old film director and actor,' said Tom. 'Used to play Nazi villains in Hollywood movies.'

Tom loved old films almost as much as old cars.

'That SS man you saw last night isn't really your father,' said Sarah consolingly. 'Any more than that happy housewife in there is your mum. They're just alternative versions. Somewhere your real dad is still trying to persuade his students that history is more exciting than sex, drugs and rock and roll. And your real mum is giving them hell on the Stock Exchange!'

'I hope so,' said Tom.

Suddenly he was overcome with longing for the real, same universe that he'd grown up in. It had its faults but it was a million times better than this.

'Do you think we'll ever get back, Sarah?'

'We will,' said Sarah determinedly. 'We must!'

'How?'

'Search me. Maybe the effect of the malfunction will suddenly wear off and we'll find ourselves where we're supposed to be!'

'I wonder what we're like?' said Tom.

'Sorry?'

'Our alternative versions. The us that grew up in this universe.' Tom waved a hand around the peaceful, sunny terrace. 'It'd be easy to get used to this, wouldn't it? What did you call it – the high life? Living in a stately home, best of everything on demand, slave-servants dancing around you. Being convinced that everyone outside your special group is just so much inferior scum, born to serve you! I don't think I'd like us if we met us!'

'You'd better hope we don't,' said Sarah practically. 'If the genuine this-universe Tom and Sarah turn up we're in trouble.'

Tom looked around. 'We'd better get moving, then.'

'Moving where?'

'Away from here. The real us are bound to turn up eventually. What do we do then?'

'Denounce them as imposters,' said Sarah cheerfully. 'We were here first!'

'We'd never get away with it.'

'It's worth a try. What's the point of just running off into the blue?'

'We could try to make contact with the resistance. They might help us.'

'What makes you think so? We didn't part on the best of terms, remember?'

Tom nodded, remembering the fierce, dark-haired girl who'd tried to shoot them in the museum corridor.

'That's why that Annis girl didn't trust us, of course – my celebrity dad. There must have been some kind of family portrait in the SS equivalent of *Hello* magazine. "Our beloved gauleiter at home in his beautiful eighteenth-century mansion with his son and niece." '

'Which means nobody else in the resistance will trust us either,' said Sarah.

Tom shook his head in despair. 'So what do we do? It's too dangerous to stay, and we've got nowhere to go! We're trapped.'

CHAPTER SIXTEEN

PRISONERS

THE DISCUSSION was interrupted by Tom's mother, who came bustling on to the terrace to see if they were all right.

'We're fine,' said Tom. 'I thought we might go for a bit of a walk.'

'Don't overdo it, will you, dear,' said his new-model mother. 'And you'll stay in the grounds, won't you?'

'Must we?'

'I'm afraid your father was most insistent. He's given instructions to all the security guards. Something to do with the political situation. I expect he's worried about those dreadful resistance people. Your father will explain it all when he gets home.' She smiled brightly at Sarah. 'We women don't understand such things, do we, dear?'

Tom grinned, and Sarah didn't reply.

'Besides, it'll be lunch-time soon,' his mother went on. 'I'm making your favourite, *Eisbein* and *sauerkraut*.'

'Wonderful,' said Tom, wondering what on earth it was.

She turned to Sarah. 'Would you like to come and help me with the dumplings, dear? I know how you love to cook. And Tom always says that nobody makes dumplings like yours, don't you, Tom?'

'I certainly do!' said Tom, struggling to keep a straight face.

Sarah's idea of cooking was to open a self-heating can of curry, and she didn't do that if she could persuade anyone else to do it!

He grinned at Sarah. 'Don't let me stand in your way if you want to get stuck in with the pots and pans.'

'I think I'd better stay and look after Tom,' said Sarah sweetly. 'I don't think he's quite himself yet.'

'How kind of you. Well, I must get back to the kitchen. I'll send one of the maids to give you a call when lunch is ready.'

'What time is Father getting back?' asked Tom.

'He said he might be home early. He's got a very important meeting this evening, here at the house. And I know he's keen to have a long chat with you both.'

I bet he is, thought Tom, and shuddered.

His mother disappeared into the house, and Tom and Sarah took a walk around the grounds. It was a fine, sunny autumn afternoon with just the slightest nip in the air to suggest the coming of winter.

They strolled around the lawns and garden and

shrubberies, all beautifully cared for. Tom remembered coming last summer, with the place full of picnicking families with little kids dashing about. It was strange having the place all to themselves.

'I suppose it was like this back in the eighteenth century,' said Tom. 'The lord of the manor strolling about and all the common people kept well out of sight.'

They checked all the exits, the ones down by the lake and the main one at the front of the house.

All were guarded by SS storm troopers, who saluted respectfully and turned them politely but firmly back.

Tom made an attempt to talk his way past one of the sentries.

'Surely the gauleiter didn't mean his orders to apply to us?'

'To you in particular, sir,' said the sentry. 'The gauleiter wants you safe at home until the political situation settles down.'

'I didn't think there were any politics here,' said Sarah as they turned away. 'I mean, with only one party . . .'

'Must be internal politics,' said Tom. 'The Nazis are great on internal feuds. The SS wiped out most of the Brownshirts back in 1930 something. That's why they still hate each other . . .'

Sarah glanced back at the sentries.

'Well, whatever the reason, it doesn't look as if we're going anywhere. We're prisoners. VIP prisoners, but prisoners all the same.'

Tom and Sarah walked back towards the terrace.

'If we're prisoners, we'll be here when my SS dad gets home,' said Tom. 'What are we going to say to him?'

'What's he going to say to us?' said Sarah. 'We'll just have to bluff it out!'

A maid came to summon them to lunch, which was served in a large and luxurious dining-room.

The three of them, Tom and Sarah and Tom's new-model mum sat at a long, polished table, big enough for a dozen diners, with servants hovering all around.

Tom discovered that *Eisbein* was boiled hock of bacon served on the bone, with pink ham nestling somewhere inside a mass of gelatinous fat. The whole thing looked pretty disgusting, but the ham, when you got to it, was delicious and the potatoes, *sauerkraut* and dumplings were OK.

Since it was supposed to be his favourite, Tom made an effort to eat as much as he could, watched anxiously by his new mother.

Sarah, who was pretty much a vegetarian, just hacked her *Eisbein* about a bit, and filled up on potatoes, *sauerkraut* and dumplings.

Her aunt didn't really seem to notice. Apparently it wasn't important what girls ate.

Dessert was something called *sachertorte*, which was chocolatey, creamy, fattening and delicious.

They were just having coffee when a long, black

limousine drew up on the terrace outside and a strange yet familiar figure got out. The car moved away.

'Oh good, your father's back,' said Tom's mother. 'He said he might come home early.'

Moments later a tall figure in SS uniform came into the room. Tom's mother jumped up and ran to meet him and he gave her a perfunctory kiss on the cheek.

She looked reprovingly at Tom and Sarah.

'Where are your manners, children? Say hello to your father properly, Tom!'

Apparently things were a bit more formal in this family.

Tom stood up and bowed stiffly. 'Good afternoon, sir.'

He nudged Sarah, who stood up and did a brief bob. 'Good afternoon, sir,' she echoed.

'Good afternoon,' said Tom's father, and waved to them to sit down. He stood, looking hard at them and Tom returned his gaze.

His father was the same and yet different, he decided. He looked leaner and fitter for a start. The face was the same but it looked stronger, the face of someone used to authority, and the grey eyes were hard and keen.

All the same, thought Tom, it was Dad all right. It was a shock, and a very unpleasant one, to see him in the black uniform of the SS.

'I've had a busy morning,' said this strange new father, 'looking into the extraordinary circumstances surrounding your return. I can't say things are very much clearer.' He looked from Tom to Sarah. 'I'll see you two in my study in ten minutes. I have a number of questions to ask. I hope for your sakes that you will be able to answer them to my satisfaction.'

He nodded to his wife, who looked terrified, and strode from the room.

'I think I'll have another piece of that tart,' said Tom. 'And some more coffee. What about you, Sarah?'

'Why not?'

Beneath his apparent calm Tom was thinking furiously and he was sure Sarah was as well. They couldn't prepare any answers because they had no idea what the questions were going to be.

They'd just have to improvise.

His new mother was looking anxiously at them. 'Are you sure you're both all right? You're acting rather strangely.'

'We're fine,' said Tom. 'Don't worry.'

'Don't keep your father waiting, will you, dear? You know what his temper's like. He's been under a lot of stress.'

Tom grinned encouragingly at Sarah. 'So have we,' he said.

He looked at the expensive-looking military watch that was part of his new outfit. 'Don't worry, he said ten minutes. We've still got three minutes left!'

They finished their coffee and tart and stood up.

Suddenly Tom realised he had no idea where the study was.

'Tell you what, Mother,' he said, 'you can escort us to the study, make sure we're not late.'

It didn't really make much sense but his new mother was far too flustered to argue. She led them out of the dining-room, along a couple of corridors, and stopped before a heavy oak door.

She looked so anxious that Tom gave her a quick kiss on the cheek. 'Don't worry, Mum,' he said. 'We'll take it from here.'

He tapped on the door and opened it, and they went inside.

They found themselves in a tall and gloomy room, filled with scattered tables and heavy, old-fashioned chairs.

A little spiral staircase led to a book-lined gallery that overlooked the room, running round three of its four walls.

The gauleiter, Tom's father, sat at a massive desk, working on some papers by the light of an old-fashioned desk lamp.

He ignored them, continuing to work on the papers.

Tom was very familiar with this tactic. It was a favourite of the headmaster at his school. It was supposed to make you nervous, but it only made Tom angry.

'We can come back later if you're busy,' he said.

The gauleiter looked up with an expression of angry surprise.

'You will get nowhere by being insolent!'

'And you'll get nowhere by trying to bully us, Uncle,' said Sarah. 'Why don't you just get on with your questions?'

This time Tom's father looked utterly astonished – presumably because Sarah was female. It must have been like a chair or a table answering back.

He looked so angry that Tom was afraid Sarah had gone too far.

With a visible effort Tom's father mastered his temper.

'What I need from you, both of you, is not impertinence, but an account of yesterday's extraordinary events.'

'We'll do our best,' said Tom. 'But I'm afraid our memories are still rather confused. The accident, you know. Sarah was badly shaken up and I got mild concussion.'

His father sat back, looking keenly at him.

'Indeed? Then let us start with a question you can surely answer without difficulty. A question about events before your accident. You both went to New Berlin to receive merit awards, for outstanding achievement in the junior division of the SS. You, Thomas, for drill and discipline, and you, Sarah, for exemplary cooking and housekeeping. You do remember that?'

Sarah gritted her teeth.

Tom said hurriedly, 'Yes, of course we do.'

The gauleiter paused. 'So why are you here? *Why did you come back a day early — missing the award ceremony altogether?*'

CHAPTER SEVENTEEN

INTERROGATION

BOWLED OUT first ball! thought Tom despairingly.

He could blame the crash for a blurred memory of recent events. But unless he claimed complete amnesia . . .

And it was a bit late for that, now he'd recognised both his parents.

His alternative-universe father, the gauleiter, was glaring at him. 'Well?'

Sarah said, 'Because you sent for us, of course.'

'I did no such thing!'

Quickly Tom picked up on Sarah's inspiration.

'You didn't send us a message?'

'Certainly not.'

'Well, we certainly got one. An urgent message, ordering us to come home at once.'

The gauleiter frowned. 'Didn't you wonder about it? Under the circumstances . . .'

'We were surprised, certainly,' said Sarah. 'But we knew you were worried about the political situation here. We thought it must be something to do with that.'

The gauleiter waved a hand. 'Sit, sit!'

Tom pulled out a chair for Sarah and another for himself. They both sat down.

'All right,' said the gauleiter. 'What happened next?'

Tom felt himself floundering again.

'Well, we arrived at the transmat terminal . . .'

'Weren't you surprised that I hadn't sent a car?'

Once again, Sarah came to the rescue.

'But you had. At least, there was an official limousine waiting for us, with an SS driver. We naturally assumed that you'd sent it.'

'I see. Well, go on. What happened next?'

'We passed out,' said Sarah.

'How? Why?'

'We just don't know. Maybe we were knocked out, maybe it was drugs, or gas . . . We just can't remember.'

Tom decided it was time to skate quickly over some very thin ice.

'We don't really remember anything after that,' he said firmly. 'I mean, there are sort of vague flashes of things but we can neither of us be sure if they were real or nightmares.'

'Did you get a look at your kidnappers? Could you identify them?'

'Not really,' said Tom. 'I know there were two, and I think one was male and the other female. But we never saw their faces, not that I remember. Either they were masked, or we were blindfolded.'

'What's the first thing you do remember?'

'Waking up in the back of the truck,' said Sarah. 'It crashed and the doors burst open. Tom was still unconscious. I managed to drag him out, I was afraid the truck would blow up.'

Nothing like a bit of the truth to bolster up a really good lie! thought Tom.

The remorseless stream of questions continued.

'Did you see any sign of the kidnappers?'

Sarah shook her head. 'No, they'd vanished. We managed to get to our feet and staggered away from the crash. We were afraid they'd come back for us.'

'Why did you run from the SS storm troopers? You must have known they wouldn't harm you. As soon as they recognised you, you would have been safe.'

'If they recognised us,' said Tom. 'They might have decided to shoot first. Besides, we didn't know who they were, not at first. We just saw lights and heard voices. We thought the kidnappers were trying to recapture us.'

'Why did you run when you did see them, in the Vale of Health?'

'We were frightened and confused,' said Sarah. 'We'd been kidnapped, drugged and we'd just survived a crash.

We didn't know what we were doing.'

The gauleiter studied their faces for a moment.

Tom and Sarah looked back as innocently as they could.

'Do you really expect me to believe this ridiculous farrago?' thundered the gauleiter.

Tom didn't – but he had to go on with the bluff. If the gauleiter decided they were imposters, he'd have them imprisoned – or shot!

'It's all we can tell you, sir,' he said virtuously. 'I know it sounds strange, but why should we lie to you? If we were making things up, we'd invent a more believable story!'

Sarah said, 'All we do know is that something very strange happened to us, and we don't really know how we ended up here.'

And that much at least is perfectly true! thought Tom.

It was clear that something in Sarah's voice carried conviction. The gauleiter started looking less angry and more worried. Started, thought Tom, to look more like his father . . .

'You said you were looking into things this morning, sir?' he said. 'Can you tell us anything about what you found out?'

'It all seems to have started sometime yesterday,' said the gauleiter. Encouragingly, he spoke in a more friendly tone. 'Two young people were observed at the Anniversary Exhibition in the Reichsmuseum. A young man and a young woman of about your age. They were making disrespectful remarks about the memory of the Fuehrer, and about the Reich itself.'

Tom decided to go on to the attack. 'And is this supposed to have been us, sir?' he demanded. 'That's absurd. Even if we held such ideas . . . '

The gauleiter looked up quickly.

'Which, of course, we don't,' Tom went on hurriedly. 'We'd scarcely wander around central London making treasonable remarks in public.'

'What happened next?' asked Sarah.

'The remarks were overheard by a loyal citizen, a certain Mrs Winter. She reported the couple to an SS policeman attached to the museum. He attempted to arrest them. The couple fled. The policeman reported the event to the nearest SS command post, and a somewhat over-zealous young SS lieutenant turned out a number of SS patrols to find the fugitives. They failed.' The gauleiter sat back in his chair looking baffled. 'It was at this point that events seemed to spiral out of control.'

'Please go on, sir,' said Tom. He was anxious to find out what had happened himself.

The gauleiter said, 'Subsequently this Lieutenant Niles decided the fugitives must be hiding in the museum and took a squad of storm troopers to look for them. When he arrived at the museum he heard two shots . . . '

Annis shooting at us, thought Tom.

'Lieutenant Niles sent patrols up to the galleries to investigate, more shots were fired and a number of SS men were either wounded or killed. An SS truck was stolen and later spotted by a Brownshirt patrolman. He reported that a young man was driving. There was a young girl with him.'

He looked hard at Tom and Sarah.

When they didn't reply he went on. 'The truck was traced to this area, and forced off the road. Shortly after that you two were found nearby. You alone, I might add. There was no trace of any kidnappers.'

The gauleiter sat back, suspicion returning to his manner. 'If you can come up with a theory that explains all that, I shall be extremely glad to hear it!'

Tom's mind was racing.

They had to come up with some kind of explanation to back up their unlikely story.

Something good enough to buy them a little time . . .

He racked his brains for his memories of Nazi history and suddenly inspiration came to him.

'You mentioned a difficult political situation, sir.'

'So?'

'Is it possible that someone high up in the Party, some rival, would want to discredit you?'

The gauleiter smiled wryly. 'I could give you a list as long as my arm!' he said unexpectedly. 'I have been associated with policies of which some of my colleagues do not approve.'

Sarah picked up on Tom's idea and developed it further. 'Suppose some of these colleagues tried to strike at you through us?'

'That's right,' said Tom. 'We're kidnapped, drugged, placed in some kind of discreditable situation.'

'Maybe they set up someone reasonably like us to impersonate us, to go around making treasonable remarks,' continued Sarah. 'The idea is for us to be picked up later on with forged evidence of guilt on us, arrested in thoroughly incriminating circumstances. If it could be made to seem as if we were involved with treason, mixed up with the resistance, it would reflect discredit on you. People would say that you must have known, that you might even be involved yourself.'

Tom rounded off the unlikely story.

'Then this lieutenant turns up unexpectedly with his squad, the kidnappers panic and flee with us in the truck. If the two who impersonated us were driving the truck, that would account for the Brownshirt's report. After the crash they panicked and abandoned us. We panicked too and ran, and the SS patrols ended up chasing us and not the kidnappers!'

The story was tissue-paper thin, thought Tom, but it had one big advantage. It played on the paranoia that had always run right through the Nazi Party. The top figures were always spying on and plotting against each other. There really had been all kinds of smear campaigns and frame-ups, people discredited and even shot on forged and faked evidence.

The idea certainly seemed to appeal to the gauleiter.

His face was alive with interest. 'It would certainly explain a great deal,' he murmured. 'And I've a damned good idea who's behind it. A scheme like this has young Himmler's dirty fingerprints all over it . . .' He stood up. 'I must investigate this further. I have an important meeting here this evening, but first thing tomorrow . . . Meanwhile you will remain at home until the situation clarifies. You have made quite enough public appearances for the moment.' Awkwardly he added, 'I wish you both a good recovery from your unpleasant experiences.'

He smiled, and just for a moment Tom saw his father again. Then the gauleiter returned.

'For now, you may go. I have work to do. I may have more questions for you later.'

Thankfully Tom and Sarah fled.

For the moment, at least, they were off the hook, thought Tom.

But for how long?

CHAPTER EIGHTEEN

DEPOSITION

AS THE widow of a senior Party official, Mrs Winter was treated with great respect when she attended Lieutenant Niles's SS command post to make her formal statement.

She dictated the deposition to an SS secretary. Afterwards Niles questioned her in detail about the young people's extraordinary remarks, and tried, without very much success, to get a more detailed description from her.

His questions and her answers were added to the statement.

While the deposition was being typed, he showed Mrs Winter the photograph file of resistance suspects. She recognised nobody, although she hesitated for a moment over the photographs of a certain brother and sister. Then she shook her head.

'No, there's some likeness, but the colouring is wrong.'

Since the statement still wasn't ready for signature,

Lieutenant Niles put the old lady in an ante-room while he got on with some work.

Minutes later he heard a shriek and the old lady erupted into his office waving a newspaper.

'It's them!' she shouted. 'I've found them. Look, here they are on the very front page of "Party News"!'

Lieutenant Niles took the paper from her and studied it.

The front-page photograph, taken outside the transmat terminal, showed Gauleiter Martin, flanked by a young man and a young woman in the uniform of the SS (Junior Branch). The caption beneath read: *Gauleiter Peter Martin says farewell to his son Thomas and his niece Sarah, as they leave for New Berlin. There they will receive their Nazi Party Junior Merit Awards from the hand of the new Fuehrer himself.*

Lieutenant Niles looked down at the old lady.

'It's impossible. Look again!'

The old lady snatched the paper from him and looked hard at the photograph.

'Impossible or not, young man, it is perfectly true. The photograph is very clear and there is nothing wrong with my eyesight or my memory.' She shook her head disgustedly. 'The children of a high Party official wandering the streets talking treason. It's disgraceful.'

'Mrs Winter, this is very important. You are absolutely certain these are the two young people you saw?'

'Positive. I'm willing to make a statement here and now.'

Niles took back the paper. 'No, not yet . . .' He lowered his voice. 'As I'm sure you can appreciate, Mrs Winter, this matter must be handled carefully. I shall give it my personal attention. When your identification is needed, I will send for you again, but for the moment I must ask you to observe complete secrecy. Say nothing to anyone – in the name of the Reich!'

The secretary returned with the typed deposition, Mrs Winter signed it and Lieutenant Niles bustled her out, swearing her to secrecy once again.

When she had gone, he shut himself up in his office and started thinking hard. The information in his poss-ession – his alone as long as that old bat kept her mouth shut – was potential dynamite. The children of the Gauleiter of Central London District involved in treason! No wonder he had taken such an interest in the affair at the Reichsmuseum. He was trying to organise a cover-up to protect his traitorous children.

The important question was, how could this infor-mation be turned to best advantage? Properly used, thought Niles exultantly, it could get him out of all the trouble he was in . . .

At first Niles considered blackmail – the Reichs-museum fiasco forgotten, promotion instead of disgrace, all this in return for his silence.

Something about the memory of the gauleiter's hard grey eyes discouraged him from this idea. It occurred to him that he had no need to deal with the matter directly.

Who in the Party would most like to get something on the gauleiter? Who was powerful enough to see that his informant was properly rewarded?

Lieutenant Niles picked up his phone.

'Gestapo HQ please . . .' After a few minutes' wait he said, 'This is Lieutenant Niles of the SS. I wish to make an immediate and urgent appointment with Commissioner Himmler. You may tell him it concerns the security of the Reich – and the Gauleiter of Central London District . . .'

Tom and Sarah were having tea on the terrace – and discussing their interview with the gauleiter.

'He believed that ridiculous story of ours because he wanted to believe it,' said Tom. 'But it won't stand up to much investigation.'

'Especially if our this-universe equivalents turn up,' said Sarah. 'It's bound to happen sooner or later. What do you think they'll do to us when they find out?'

'Shoot us, I imagine,' said Tom gloomily. 'That or lock us up and lose the key. They'll never believe the truth. Besides, it would be too embarrassing to have two pairs of us around.' He sighed. 'It's a good job he's got this urgent meeting tonight to keep him busy. We'll have to escape in the night and go on the run again.'

Sarah shook her head. 'First I want to go to that meeting.'

Tom stared at her. 'Whatever for?'

'I don't know, I just do. There was something about the way he talked about it.'

'What do you mean?'

'The look in his eye, the way he got tense whenever he mentioned it. He looked worried. Guilty even.'

'Guilty of what?'

'I just have the feeling that the this-universe version of your dad and my uncle is up to something shady.'

'Suppose he is? What good does that do us?'

'Knowledge is power,' said Sarah impressively. 'If we can find out what it is, maybe we can use it to put pressure on him, stop him from turning us in. He's a very powerful man, remember, and we stand a much better chance of surviving with him on our side.'

Tom wasn't too keen on the idea of blackmailing his own father. Then again, the gauleiter wasn't really his father – well, he was and he wasn't – and what Sarah said made a lot of sense.

'He could put us in touch with this universe's top transmat scientists,' Sarah went on. 'Maybe they could find some way of getting us home.'

'Don't get too carried away just yet,' said Tom sternly. 'This wonderful plan of yours depends on two things. Firstly on our discovering that Dad – the gauleiter – really is up to something. Secondly, on our getting into this top-secret meeting.'

'The first depends on the second,' Sarah pointed out.

'So how do we manage it?' Tom replied. 'I don't suppose he'll invite us . . .'

'Where do you think he's going to have this meeting?'

'In the study, I suppose. The one where we played twenty questions after lunch.'

'Exactly. And that study has an upper level, a sort of gallery lined with bookshelves. So, tonight after dinner, we plead tiredness and go off for an early night. They'll be glad to get rid of us anyway. Then we sneak into the study before the meeting and hide ourselves up in that gallery! Nothing to it!'

'Oh yes, dead simple,' said Tom satirically. 'If Dad really has got something to hide, if they have the meeting in the study and not somewhere else, if we can sneak in without getting seen . . . It can hardly go wrong!'

Surprisingly enough, it didn't.

Not at first anyway . . .

CHAPTER NINETEEN

SECRETS AFTER DINNER

'YOUR FATHER has important dinner guests,' Tom's mother announced fussily when they went back into the house.

'That's nice,' said Tom cautiously. 'Who are they?'

'There's Mr Kennedy, the American ambassador – a most charming man. He's the great-grandson of Joseph Kennedy, you know, who was American ambassador when Great Britain first joined the Reich. And General Wolff of the Brownshirts is coming as well. The general is a little difficult socially. I think he's rather shy. But your father seems to enjoy his company. We've seen a good deal of him recently.'

'Sounds like a wonderful evening,' said Sarah.

Mrs Martin looked anxiously at them. 'You will be on your best behaviour, won't you?' She turned to Sarah. 'And wear something nice. The general has a weakness for pretty girls.'

Sarah tried to grit her teeth and smile at the same time. 'I'll do my best.'

'We'll all have to take ourselves off after dinner,' Mrs Martin went on. 'The men are having some kind of meeting in the study.'

'Fine,' said Sarah. 'I was planning on an early night . . .'

The dinner passed off surprisingly well.

The American ambassador's name was Michael Kennedy. He was slim, tanned and white-haired, a well-preserved sixty-something. He had the diplomat's gift of producing an endless flow of smalltalk on any and every subject.

General Wolff, on the other hand, was a bullet-headed ox of a man who hardly spoke at all, devoting himself to chomping his way through everything put in front of him – which was a great deal.

Dinner was an elaborate affair of many courses, served by an impressive array of servants in the room where they'd had lunch.

Tom and Sarah, all dressed up in their best, sat up straight, ate small mouthfuls, and spoke when they were spoken to, which wasn't often. Seen and not heard seemed to be the rule as far as they were concerned.

As soon as the pudding course was over, Sarah stood up. 'Will you excuse me if I don't stay for coffee? I'm feeling rather tired.'

(They'd arranged that Sarah should leave early to set up pillow-dummies in both their beds.)

Tom hung on for a little while longer after she'd left.

Then he too stood up. 'I'll go to bed as well, if you don't mind, sir. Bit of a headache . . .'

The gauleiter nodded, and Tom left the table.

Mrs Martin accompanied him to the door.

'Are you feeling all right?'

'I'm fine, really,' said Tom. 'We both need a good night's sleep. Will you ask the servants not to disturb either of us until tomorrow?'

Mrs Martin promised she would and returned to her guests.

As soon as the door closed behind her, Tom headed for the study. Sarah was already waiting by the door. They went inside, climbed the spiral staircase to the gallery and lay flat on the floor.

'Any chance they'll spot us?' whispered Tom.

'I don't think so. We're in deep shadow up here.'

They settled down to wait.

After what seemed an age they heard voices outside the study.

The door opened, and the gauleiter came in, followed by General Wolff and the American ambassador.

Peering from the gallery they saw the gauleiter settle his guests on chairs and serve them brandy.

They heard the gauleiter's voice. 'If you will be patient

for a few moments, gentlemen, I'll summon the last two members of our group. For obvious reasons their arrival had to be a little more – discreet.'

They saw the gauleiter open the study curtains, revealing French windows giving on to the terrace. He lifted his desk lamp and moved it to and fro three times. He put down the lamp and waited. A few minutes later, two figures slipped through the open French windows.

Tom and Sarah looked at each other wide-eyed. To their silent amazement, they recognised both newcomers.

One was the young man called Mark, the other was the girl Annis. The two members of the resistance they'd met at the museum.

If Tom and Sarah were surprised, Mark and Annis were even more astonished.

At the sight of the gauleiter, Mark jumped back in alarm. 'What is this, a trap?' His hand slid inside his coat.

The gauleiter smiled. 'Surely you knew this is my house?'

'Yes, of course,' said Annis. 'But we thought we'd be meeting someone in your household. A servant, perhaps. We never dreamed it would be *you*!'

The gauleiter stepped forward, raising his hand.

'Please, there's no need for alarm. I believe you were summoned here for your first face-to-face meeting with someone you call the Leader.'

'That's right,' said Annis. Her hand too was inside her

coat. 'Where is he? Have you arrested him?'

The gauleiter said, 'You have found him. I am the Leader. This is the big city – you want to watch your step!'

Mark said, 'Perhaps – but I find the country too quiet.'

It was obviously an exchange of passwords.

Annis stared at the gauleiter unbelievingly. 'The leader really is *you* . . .?'

'Me,' said the gauleiter calmly.

Mark said, 'But you've been hunting us for years.'

The gauleiter smiled. 'Yes, indeed. I had to keep up appearances. But I never caught you, did I? There was always the last-minute tip-off.' He waved towards the others. 'This is General Wolff of the Brownshirts. His men never quite managed to catch you either. And this gentleman is the American ambassador, Mr Michael Kennedy. We have, all three, been your collaborators – even though you didn't know who we were. Please – sit down and join us. Can I get you something to drink?'

Mark and Annis sat down, though both refused drinks.

Tom jabbed Sarah in the ribs. 'Good old Dad,' he whispered. 'I was right about him all along – even this version. He's not only *in* the resistance, he's in charge of it!'

The gauleiter took his place behind his big desk.

'Since Britain was conquered, seventy-five years ago, much has changed. The grip of the Nazi regime is beginning to weaken here in Britain and the people of this country want their freedom again. We have grown weary of Nazi tyranny. Meanwhile, the Nazi rule of mainland Europe has grown steadily more repressive.' The gauleiter paused, studying the two young resistance workers. 'I have taken the risk of asking you to come here so that we can inform you of a most important project – the separation of Province Britannica from the Reich!'

There was a stunned silence from Annis and Mark.

Then Annis said, 'But won't the Reich simply re-invade, conquer Britain all over again?'

The gauleiter smiled. 'Mr Ambassador?'

The American ambassador said, 'America has grown increasingly concerned about the abuse of human rights in Europe – and the increasingly aggressive attitude of the Nazi Reich towards the United States. Something has to be done. As a first step, we have agreed to recognise an independent Province Britannica, renamed Great Britain, once it separates itself from the Reich. It is our belief that an alliance with America will stand in the way of a fresh invasion of England.'

Mark was still looking stunned. 'You said "As a first step"?'

The ambassador said, 'We hope that the restoration of freedom to Britain will one day lead to similar results in mainland Europe. It may take years, but one day we shall succeed.'

'It's a wonderful idea,' said Mark. 'Wonderful!'

'Can you really do it?' asked Annis. 'Split Britain off from the Reich?'

'We can try,' said the gauleiter. 'Some, though not all, of my SS colleagues are sympathetic. General Wolff and his Brownshirts, long despised and undervalued, have pledged their support. And then there's your resistance organisation. Our main problem, of course, is Commissioner Himmler of the Gestapo. As you know, he's a descendant of the original Himmler, and never lets anyone forget it. A fanatical Nazi with spies everywhere – and he hates my guts.'

General Wolff said, 'My Brownshirts will deal with him and his spies when the time comes.'

A voice rang out from the French windows. 'Your time will never come, traitors. You are all under arrest.'

Peering down, Tom and Sarah saw a young SS officer step into the room through the French windows, a revolver in his hand.

The gauleiter said, 'Lieutenant Niles! How dare you interrupt my guests like this? Aren't you in enough trouble already?'

'You're the one in trouble, Herr Gauleiter,' said the lieutenant sneeringly.

'Really?' The gauleiter sounded bored. 'Just what do you think you're doing?'

'Arresting a nest of traitors – traitors plotting high treason!'

'All on your own? I take it you want to grab all the glory. Isn't that a little over-ambitious?'

'I won't be alone for long,' said Niles. 'The Gestapo are on the way. You were already under suspicion and once I told them I had positive proof that your children were traitors . . .'

'Proof?' said the gauleiter sharply. 'What kind of proof?'

'Mrs Winter recognised their photographs in the "Party News". The subversives she reported are your son and your niece. She's prepared to swear to it.'

'You call that proof?' said the gauleiter scornfully. 'The word of an obsessive old woman?'

'It's enough to get you arrested by the Gestapo, you and all your family. They'll find more evidence, get confessions out of you . . .'

In the gallery, Tom and Sarah were looking at each other in horror. Everything had been going so well, and now this idiot was going to ruin everything.

Something had to be done.

Tom nodded to Sarah, swung himself over the low rail at the edge of the gallery and dropped on top of Niles, bearing him to the ground.

Niles's head thumped against the wooden floor and he groaned and collapsed.

Tom scrambled to his feet. 'Sorry to interrupt, sir, but I thought it was time to intervene.'

Sarah came down the spiral staircase to join him.

Mark and Annis stared at them both in amazement. 'You!'

The gauleiter said, 'You know each other?'

'There's no time to go into that now,' said Tom. 'Not if the Gestapo are on the way! You two had better clear off.'

'You're right,' said the gauleiter. He turned to Annis and Mark. 'Leave the way you came. I'll get in touch as soon as it's safe. Don't argue, just go!'

Mark and Annis slipped out of the open French window.

The gauleiter turned to his other guests. 'I advise you to leave as well. The Gestapo have nothing on either of you yet, but perhaps you'd better be gone when they arrive. If I get out of this alive, I'll contact you as soon as I can.'

General Wolff looked down at Niles. He bent down and picked up the unconscious man's revolver.

'What about him?'

'Take him with you and lock him up somewhere, I'll deal with him later.'

Dragging Niles between them, the ambassador and the Brownshirt general hurried out.

The gauleiter turned to Tom. 'And now, young man . . .'

Mrs Martin hurried into the room.

'Peter, dear, what's happening? The general and the ambassador have just rushed off without a word, dragging some unfortunate young man with them.'

'Please, dear, not now,' said the gauleiter patiently. 'I'll explain later – you've come at a rather tricky moment . . .'

'You don't know how tricky,' said his wife with unexpected spirit. 'The Gestapo are at the main gates, demanding admission.'

'Yes, yes, I was expecting them.'

'There's something else,' announced Mrs Martin.

The gauleiter said, 'It's hard to imagine what else *could* happen this evening! Well?'

'There's a message from transmat HQ that Tom and Sarah have arrived safely from New Berlin. Since there was nobody there to meet them the transmat people provided a car, so Tom and Sarah will be home at any minute.' She looked at the Tom and Sarah who were standing in front of her. 'And that's impossible – isn't it?'

CHAPTER TWENTY

SHOWDOWN

'I'M NOT sure I know what's possible and what isn't any more,' said the gauleiter grimly. 'All right, leave it to me, dear, I'll deal with it.'

Obediently Mrs Martin hurried away.

Tom looked despairingly at Sarah. 'Now what?'

'There may be a way out of this,' she said.

'I'd be very glad to hear it,' said the gauleiter.

'The main problem is this old lady who's identified us as being the two people everyone was after yesterday? If you can discredit her testimony, you'll be in the clear?'

The gauleiter nodded. 'The Gestapo may be suspicious of me but they have no real proof. Mrs Winter's deposition, identifying you two as traitors, gives them a foot in the door. Without it, they're powerless.'

'Right,' said Sarah. 'Forget about us, we don't exist. Give us time to get out of sight, and let the Gestapo in.'

'And what do I tell them?'

'Just stall them until your children – your real children – arrive.'

'I take it you two are not my real son and niece?'

'Well, yes and no,' said Tom.

'Not really,' said Sarah.

'Then who the devil are you?'

'Later,' said Sarah. 'Now, here's what you do . . .'

Tom and Sarah were back in hiding, stretched out on the gallery floor.

They watched as the gauleiter ushered a small ratty-looking man in a black leather overcoat into the room.

The newcomer was accompanied by two very large and thuggish-looking men, also in black leather coats, who took up positions by the door.

The Gauleiter gestured towards the drinks cabinet. 'May I offer you some refreshment, Commissioner Himmler? A whisky, perhaps? Brandy? A cigar?'

'I follow the example of our revered Fuehrer, Adolf the First, in abstaining completely from both alcohol and tobacco.'

'Yes, of course, I'd forgotten,' said the gauleiter, who'd done no such thing. 'Then what can I do for you – at this rather unusual hour?'

'You have been entertaining visitors?'

'Yes indeed. General Wolff and the American ambassador, both old friends of mine.'

'An unusual mixture. What was the purpose of this
meeting?'

'Purely social,' said the gauleiter smoothly.

'I see. Well, perhaps we can discuss that later. I am
sorry to inform you, Herr Gauleiter, that serious charges
have been laid against members of your family.'

'And who makes these charges?'

'A certain Lieutenant Niles – one of your own men!'

Commissioner Himmler looked round. 'Incidentally,
where is Lieutenant Niles? He was to meet me here.'

'Lieutenant Niles is under arrest. He broke in here in
a hysterical condition and threatened my guests.'

'Lieutenant Niles is an important witness, essential to
my case. You will release him immediately!'

The gauleiter's voice hardened. 'I think not,
commissioner. As you yourself pointed out, Lieutenant
Niles is one of my own men – a member of the SS, under
my command. Several charges are pending against him,
and I shall deal with him myself.'

Commissioner Himmler choked back his rage.

'You need not think you can dispose of the evidence
against your family by getting rid of Niles. We have
another witness.'

The gauleiter yawned. 'Indeed. A witness to what?'

'We have positive proof that your son and your niece

160

have been indulging in subversive behaviour. We strongly suspect that they were concerned in a later incident in the Reichsmuseum – causing the deaths of several SS men.'

'Lieutenant Niles was largely responsible for those deaths. I have already informed him that he faces an official enquiry. No doubt that is why he is making false and malicious charges against me.'

'We shall leave Lieutenant Niles aside for the moment,' announced Commissioner Himmler.

The gauleiter bowed. 'Willingly.'

'To return to the charges against your son and your niece . . . Charges, Herr Gauleiter, which reflect very seriously on you.'

The gauleiter yawned again. 'Forgive me, commissioner. These misdeeds of which my son and niece are accused . . . When are they supposed to have taken place?'

'Late yesterday afternoon and early yesterday evening.'

'You surprise me, commissioner, you really do. It scarcely seems possible.'

'And why not? Just because the charges concern your family?'

'No, no, for quite another reason. Because . . .' the gauleiter broke off. 'Ah, there you are! I trust you had a satisfactory trip?'

From their vantage point in the gallery, Tom and Sarah saw two young people enter the study.

Or rather, they saw themselves.

This Tom and Sarah wore a version of SS uniform. Black tunic, trousers and jackboots for the young man, black tunic, skirt and stockings for the girl.

Both had silver swastikas in their lapels.

'A right pair of young Nazis!' whispered Sarah.

'I said we wouldn't like us if we met us,' whispered Tom.

The gauleiter said, 'Commissioner Himmler, allow me to present my son Thomas and my niece Sarah.'

The young man clicked his heels and the girl bobbed in a curtsey.

'I want you to do something for me,' said the gauleiter.

'At your orders, Father.'

'Of course, Uncle.'

'Tell Commissioner Himmler where you were yesterday. In particular during late afternoon and early evening.'

'That's easy, Father. We were at the award ceremony in New Berlin, getting our Merit Awards.'

The young man pointed proudly to the order in his lapel. 'I received an award for drill and discipline.'

'And I a special award for cooking and housekeeping,' said the girl. 'In the evening we went to a reception and then to the award dinner,' she went on. 'We met several ministers – and even shook hands with the new Fuehrer himself! Just think – we touched the hand of Adolf the Third, grandson of Adolf the First!'

Commissioner Himmler's voice rose hysterically. 'You can prove this?'

'Without difficulty,' said the young man stiffly. 'Many important Party officials were present. Most of them were kind enough to talk with us, and send their good wishes to my father.'

'Also, many photographs were taken,' said the girl. 'We were in nearly all of them. I even had my picture taken with the Fuehrer!'

'So you see, commissioner,' said the gauleiter coldly, 'whatever Lieutenant Niles or Mrs Winter may say, any strange incidents that took place here in London yesterday afternoon and evening cannot possibly concern either my son or my niece.'

Commissioner Himmler made no reply.

'I take it then we can consider this incident closed?' said the Gauleiter. 'Unless you propose to transmat to New Berlin and interrogate the Fuehrer himself, and most of his ministers?'

Commissioner Himmler gave a jerky little bow. 'Naturally, the incident is now closed.'

The gauleiter just looked at him.

'My apologies,' said Commissioner Himmler stiffly.

'In writing, if you please,' said the gauleiter. 'A simple handwritten note will suffice – just for the official files.'

Commissioner Himmler bowed again and turned and marched from the room, followed by his two thugs.

Up in the gallery, Tom whispered, 'It worked! Well done, Sarah.'

They heard the gauleiter's voice. 'All right, you two, come down!'

Tom and Sarah looked at each other. Then they obeyed. There didn't seem to be anything else to do.

They descended the spiral staircase and faced their other selves.

Two Toms and two Sarahs stared at each other in mutual astonishment.

The gauleiter looked from one pair to the other.

'Now, we really must have some explanations,' he said. He looked at his son and niece — his real son and niece, immaculate in their SS uniforms. 'But first, why don't you shake hands with your other selves?'

Obediently they put out their hands.

Their other selves reached out to take them.

As the two pairs of fingers touched, the two newcomers faded away into nothingness.

Only the two uniformed figures remained.

The gauleiter wasn't to have his explanations after all.

CHAPTER TWENTY-ONE

EPILOGUE

TOM AND Sarah found themselves sitting on a bench in Trafalgar Square. To Tom's vast relief the fountain was playing, the square was full of pigeons and the buildings were all back the way he remembered them.

There was no traffic, the tourists seemed to come in all shapes, sizes and colours, and there were no swastikas. He could even see a flash of red, white and blue on a distant flagpole.

'What happened?' asked Tom dazedly.

'Search me,' said Sarah. 'It must have had something to do with meeting our other selves. Maybe we can't both exist in the same universe – not so close together, anyway. It was all right while they were in Germany, but when we ended up in the same room, shaking hands . . .'

'But how did it happen without a transmat cubicle?'

'I think we were always linked to the transmat beam in

some way, even in another dimension. Meeting our other selves was all wrong, so the transmat snatched us up again to correct things.'

'Well, so long as it *did* happen . . .' said Tom.

His mind went back over their recent adventure. 'The Gestapo ended up looking pretty silly,' he said, 'thanks to your brilliant idea. Fancy realising that our other selves would have a perfect alibi which could get us and the gauleiter off the hook.' He paused. 'Do you think he'll get away with his plan?'

'Separating Britain from the Reich? Let's hope so. Maybe things could get back on course again. What a terrible place!'

'Yes, but what a terrific chap,' said Tom.

'Who?'

'The gauleiter. Your uncle. My dad. Playing both ends against the middle, running the SS and the resistance, plotting with the Brownshirts and the Americans to fool the Nazis. I was so proud of him . . . I wish I'd had a chance to tell him so.'

Sarah nodded. 'Me too. Still, I'm glad we're home. Nice to see good old Nelson back where he belongs.'

Tom glanced up at the figure on top of the tall column and frowned. Surely . . .

An odd-looking old gent in a long cloak came and sat on their bench. He was clutching a telescope.

'Excuse me, sir,' said Tom politely. 'Could I borrow your telescope?'

'*Parlez francais, jeune homme,*' said the old man. '*C'est la règle.*'

'What did he say?' whispered Tom.

'He told you to speak French. He said it's the rule.'

Another eccentric, thought Tom. Still, better humour him.

He struggled to remember his rusty French.

'*Voulez-vous me prêter votre* – what's the French for telescope?'

'*Télescope,*' said Sarah.

'. . . *votre télescope, s'il vous plaît?*'

'*Volontiers!*' said the old man. He held out the telescope.

'I take it that's a yes,' said Tom. He took the telescope, trained it on the top of the column and adjusted the focus.

The figure on the column sprang into sharp relief.

The figure with the tricorne hat, one hand inside its coat.

Slowly, very slowly, Tom closed the telescope, and handed it back to the old man.

'*Merci,*' he said.

'*De rien,*' said the old man. '*Vive l'Empereur!*'

'*Oui,*' said Tom. '*Vive l'Empereur!*'

Sarah looked suspiciously at him. 'What's the matter, Tom? That is Nelson up there, isn't it?'

'Not exactly.'

'Then who . . .'

Tom drew a deep breath. 'Sarah,' he said gently.

'What?'

'Did you ever hear of a chap called Napoleon?'

Also by Terrance Dicks, available from Piccadilly Press:

THE UNEXPLAINED:

1 – THE WOLLAGONG INCIDENT

The first assignment Matt and his father are given is in Australia where aliens were alleged to have landed in the desert.

While Professor Stirling thinks it's just another hoax, Matt is not so sure. From what he sees and hears from the locals, he realises that something strange did happen. But not even he could have believed how strange . . .

2 – THE BERMUDA TRIANGLE INCIDENT

When an aircraft full of VIPs goes missing in the Bermuda Triangle, Matt and Professor Stirling are called on their   second assignment.

Evidence suggests paranormal activity in the area and Matt makes renewed contact with the aliens he met in Australia. But why are they being so hostile? And what secrets lurk   at the bottom of the sea, which they're not meant to discover . . . ?

3 – THE CIRCLE OF DEATH INCIDENT

Matt and his father are called once again on a desperately urgent investigation into paranormal activity. This time it's at Stonehenge. The ancient monuments have always inspired a sense of mystery and sometimes unease, but now they seem to be generating a more threatening force. Is this something that the aliens are causing, or is the whole   problem much more complex?

Matt believes that the aliens are a force for good, but as things develop, he begins to have his doubts.

4 – THE BORLEY RECTORY INCIDENT

The Borley Rectory used to be called the most haunted house in England. An unexplained fire left the rectory ruined and desolate, and for years there have been strange happenings and mysterious sightings. But when Matt and Professor Stirling investigate, they find a new explanation for the strange activity, and it is more threatening than anyone had imagined.

BOYS BEHAVING BADLY

Jeremy Daldry

An essential, crazy guide to being a boy, and all the things that are important to boys, like:

girls . . . looking sharp . . . girls . . . snogs . . . girls . . . smelly farts . . . girls . . . football and girls!

So for those of you who want to know –

how to kiss
how to ask that girl out on a date
how to get rid of spots
what is going on with your body!
how to cope with pesky little brothers
how to look cool when you're feeling hassled

and how to get around all the other problems of being a teenager, this is the book for you!

If you would like more information about books available from Piccadilly Press and how to order them, please contact us at:

Piccadilly Press Ltd
5 Castle Road
London
NW1 8PR

Fax: 0171 267 4493